A Summer's Worth of Shame

A Novel by
Colby Rodowsky

A Summer's Worth of Shame

Franklin Watts / New York / London /
Toronto / Sydney / 1980

Library of Congress Cataloging in Publication Data

Rodowsky, Colby F
A summer's worth of shame.

SUMMARY: Though Thad has always enjoyed
previous summers at the beach, this year everything is overshadowed by the shame he feels over
his father's being in prison.
[1. Fathers and sons—Fiction. 2. Prisoners'
families—Fiction] I. Title.
PZ7.R6185Su   [Fic]   79–23278
ISBN 0–531–04110–7

Also by Colby Rodowsky

WHAT ABOUT ME?
P.S. WRITE SOON
EVY-IVY-OVER

This book is for
Liz Wildberger
and
Gloria DeMarco

A Summer's Worth of Shame

CHAPTER 1

Thadeus St. Clair wanted Peter Hunter not to come.

It wasn't so much that Thad *didn't want* Peter to come, but rather that he wanted Peter himself not to be able to come.

He wanted the thread to break, unraveling crazily like line off a reel.

He wanted Peter to stay in Virginia, in that shadowed part of the winter world with which Thad was unfamiliar, wanted him to continue on with his September-to-July existence which always hovered on the outskirts of August.

He wanted this best of summer friendships to end.

It was as though Thad had been pushing his feet against this day all summer long. He had willed it not to come, knowing full well that it would arrive the way exams and dentist appointments always did. Yet, somehow, he was unprepared.

He had walked into Kellam's Market, hot and sticky from the beach, to get a root beer.

"Thad—oh Thad, back here by the potato chips," the woman had called.

Thad blinked against the sudden darkness of the store after the glaring outside light. He saw Mrs. Hunter moving towards him in silhouette.

"Hi Thad. We're here, or, at least, I am. Drove down today. Peter's on his way with his father on the boat—due in some time this evening. Hope the weather holds. Wait'll you see the *Sea Hunter*. Had it painted over the winter. It really looks. . . ."

Thad squinched and unsquinched his toes against the cold tile floor. He studied the stacks of soda cans on the shelf next to him, counting the layers of Coke and root beer and Tab unconsciously, tabulating them as a kind of defense against the woman's words.

Mrs. Hunter chattered on, waving a bag of green onion potato chips. "Peter can't wait to see you and get back to all your old haunts. Guess it wouldn't be summer if I didn't see you two boys together. Now tell me, how's everybody? Your mother and—"

"OK. Everybody's OK," said Thad prodding a flattened piece of gum with his big toe.

2

"Fine, fine. Tell your mother I'm here. I'll see her out on the dock later on, and you be watching for the boat. Anytime after seven I figure, depending on what time they got away."

Thad backed down the aisle to the front of the store. "See you, Mrs. Hunter." He pushed the money across the counter and went out into the summer heat, the root beer can burning cold against his clenched fingers.

He stood for a few minutes staring through the plate glass window, watching Peter's mother as she gathered cans and boxes into her basket. He heard a rerun of her conversation and his own slurred answers, then seemed to see his might-have-been answers running along the window like a news bulletin strung across the bottom of a TV screen:

"OK. Everybody's OK. Swell, in fact. We're all just great. Bridget just goes along pretending it's an everyday kind of summer and working at the Crab House. And Muppy, you remember my little sister, Muppy, don't you Mrs. Hunter? Well, there she is—this kid with a big, fat book of Grimm's fairy tales, reading one a day, and that's the way she counts the days until. . . . As if that book was an abacus and she was pushing big, fat beads along —story, story, story—push, push, push. And my mom's great too, except she's working as a cashier at the Beach House, which is OK I guess, except she looks tired a lot and sometimes I hear her walking around the house at night really late. And me, I watch Muppy, I mean really watch, like take care of her, just me and a ten-year-old kid. Oh, and I almost forgot, Mrs. Hunter—there's my father. I mean he's in jail, Mrs. Hunter. Doesn't everybody know that?"

Thad unzipped the top of the can and dropped the ring into the litter can. He heard it ping against the bottom and turned and walked up the street. He walked past the firehouse with its open doors and the giant red trucks crouched inside; past the library and the municipal tennis courts; past a motel and the Presbyterian church. He dropped the untasted can of root beer into the next trash can and headed home.

He walked around the side of the house, running his fingers against the weathered gray wood, and stepped out onto the dock. He stood for a minute looking at the bay, watching the blazing heat that seemed to ricochet around him. Thad flopped down on the plastic chaise, yowled sharply, and rolled off onto the dock, landing on all fours. He waited there a moment listening to the sound of his voice as it bounced off the silence. Hopping, first on one foot and then the other, he went out onto the pier, bringing his feet down hard and heavy and feeling the pier shudder beneath him. He uncoiled the hose and squirted the backs of his legs. At first the water ran hot, from the sun, and the hose felt like soft licorice in his hand.

4

As the water grew colder, the hose stiffened and Thad held it over his head and let the water stream over him as he jumped up and down. Pounding his chest with his other hand, he yelled and gargled and spit and sputtered as the water sluiced down around him. He turned off the hose and the silence returned, except for the drip of water through the boards of the pier and into the bay.

He scooped up a beach towel and shook it, listening to the pinpricks of sand as they hit the water below; then spread the towel over the chaise and flopped back down, this time on his stomach.

"There," he said. Then, clearing his throat, "There," again.

Thad looked over his shoulder quickly to make sure there was still no one around.

"Or rather, here, here, here." Like the tree in the forest, he thought. If no one hears it fall, does it make a noise? No one hears me, but I'm here, I make a noise.

"There," said Thad again, loudly.

He closed his eyes and let the leftover bits of sunlight dance and explode behind his lids. Already he could feel the steam rising off his back, could feel himself dry, could feel the sun chewing into him.

Thad loved it back on the bay, particularly at this time of day when the sun was in the west, hot and blazing orange, driving most people inside or three blocks away to the ocean beach.

At almost any other time the bayside was alive

with the comings and goings of boats and people, starting early in the morning with the throb of the large fishing boats, and ending late at night with the shreds of music that came from the club across the inlet. And winding loosely around the whole day was the hum of powerboats up and down the bay. Off in the corner of his consciousness Thad heard one now, the drone of the motor getting further and further away.

Thad tried to blank his mind, to concentrate only on the slap of the water against the bulkhead and the insistent cry of the gulls. But his mind kept coming back, darting at thoughts the way his tongue had poked at a wobbly tooth when he was small.

Peter was coming back. Peter, with whom he had shared every August for as far back as either one of them could remember, was coming tonight. Peter was that special kind of summer friend, one for exploring dunes and catching crabs, for riding the waves and the Ferris wheel. They had picked up their friendship every summer on the last week-end of July, when the Hunters arrived, starting again in midsentence, as it were, and continuing through until Labor Day. Then every fall Thad and Peter had gone back to their own homes and their own towns, to their winter selves, knowing that summer would come again and it would be good.

Thad lifted his head and looked across the in-let to the marina. He saw the empty slip where the

Sea Hunter always docked, saw it huge and waiting. In his mind he saw the boat as it came up the Chesapeake Bay and through the C & D Canal, out into the ocean and down the shore to the larger inlet, with Peter aboard. And Thad felt as though he were being invaded.

All summer Thad had tried to protect himself, to build a kind of wall around himself: taking care of Muppy more than he had to; avoiding the other summer kids and staying out of their ball games and conversations; pretending all the time that his father was not in jail, that things were as they always had been. The pretending seemed to shatter around him: even now Peter was on the *Sea Hunter* as it throbbed its way closer and closer to the marina.

And Thad wondered how he could tell him, how he could not tell him.

Thad was suddenly aware of the sting of the sun on the backs of his knees: the drawing up of skin as though a hundred tiny threads were gathering and tightening.

Opening his eyes, he blinked at the heat and the light and fumbled along the boards with his hands, looking for a towel to throw over his legs. He reached for Muppy's towel, bunched under the chaise, and shook it, turning loose a spray of sand and shells and rubber flip-flop shoes and the large, heavy book that fell with a leaden thud on the dock.

Face up, weathered and worn and water-spotted, the *Two Hundred Favorite Grimm's Fairy Tales,* with which Muppy counted off the days until their father came home, seemed to leer up at him. The book mocked and taunted him, tearing at his defenses, just as the steadily approaching *Sea Hunter* tore at them and sent them crashing down around him.

Suddenly he wanted to race out to the end of the pier, feeling it quiver beneath him, and hurl the book into the deepest part of the channel. He wanted to wait while the gulls swooped and dived and pulled at the book, tearing it to bits page by page and leaving the binding to be caught in the current and dragged out of the inlet into the greater body of the bay.

"Oh good, there it is," said Muppy, jumping over Thad where he still lay on the chaise, her legs making little trails of air across his back.

"I was afraid I'd left it on the beach. Afraid I'd have to go all the way back. And Thad, guess what? I saw Mrs. Hunter, and she said Peter's coming tonight. Aren't you glad?"

"Couldn't matter much, the book I mean, the way you leave it lying around in soppy wet towels with grungy flip-flops and all." Thad propped himself up on his elbows and stared up at his sister, who was balancing herself on two arms of a sand chair. Her glasses had slipped down on her nose and her straw-colored hair stuck out all around her head.

8

She looked tough and defenseless all at the same time, thought Thad, and his next words pushed themselves out almost in spite of himself.

"Think I'll throw it in the bay and let the gulls eat it, like they do the rest of the garbage."

"No Thad, stop it," and Muppy leaped off the chair, sending it spinning perilously close to the edge of the dock. She swooped down and grabbed the book, popping her finger into the place where it fell open, like someone replacing a cork in a bottle. Then, plucking her towel off the back of her brother's legs, she jumped over him again and went through the screen door that opened onto the dock, calling from the inside out, "And Mom says supper's ready—now. You wouldn't anyway . . . throw the book . . . you know you wouldn't, cause when it's done, all two hundred stories, then'll be the time for—"

"It won't. You don't know that," said Thad, hurling a "flip-flop" at the screen. "When the book's done, the book's done is all—and so what?"

He looked at the empty spot where Muppy had stood. He was angry with her for thinking that a story-a-day could make their father come home. He was angry with his father for being where he was, for doing what he had done. And something cold took hold of Thad.

Maybe Peter already knew. Maybe the Virginia papers had carried the same story—the same boldface type. . . .

Thad closed his eyes and saw again the city papers. "A POSITION OF TRUST . . . ," the headlines had shrieked, because the name Thadeus Brook St. Clair made headlines shriek. "SCION OF OLD, PROMINENT FAMILY . . . EMBEZZLEMENT . . . U.S. Attorney says. . . ."

A cupful of cold water hit him suddenly on the back as Muppy leaned over the upstairs porch rail yelling, "I told you supper was ready."

"Hey, cut it out," he shouted up at her.

"You deserved it, Thad. You really did. Come on now, it's spaghetti."

Pulling a shirt on, he headed through the first floor, where the bedrooms were, and up the stairs, feeling suddenly hungry.

The living room was dim, shadowed by the roll-down shade on the porch that let in thin strips of light on either side. Muppy lay on the tile floor, her chin propped in her hands, staring at the television set that spit words and numbers in a steady blue-gray stream across the screen.

"OK, Tru-weather, what's happening in East Oshkosh?" asked Thad, poking her with his foot and rolling his eyes at his mother.

"A low-pressure system, barometer falling, intermittent thunderstorms. Not in East Oshkosh but here, or sort of, down the coast, followed by probable—"

"Come on, Muppy. That's enough," said Ellen St. Clair, handing the bowl of spaghetti to Thad to

10

put on the table. "Turn that television off and let's eat. I don't know why I fooled with spaghetti, as hot as it is. We should have just had tuna."

"We always have tuna—ought to have crabs."

"At the price of crabs this summer you ought to take yourselves crabbing. It'd be something for you and Muppy to do one day. Just get some string and chicken necks and take the net. Muppy tells me Peter's coming tonight; you could all go."

"Can we, Thad? Tomorrow maybe?" Muppy asked, shoveling a second helping of spaghetti onto her plate.

"What about the intermittent thundershowers?" her brother asked, rocking back on two legs of his chair. "You'd be so busy looking at the sky you'd probably fall in the water. Or else you'd want to come home so you could check with Tru-weather on TV. It's bad enough just getting you to the beach."

"What?" asked his mother. "Muppy loves the beach."

"Sure she does, as long as the sky's one hundred percent blue with no clouds in sight. Ye gods, she reads all those stories with witches boiling people and turning everybody into toads and stuff, but she's afraid of weather. Just dumb old weather."

"I'm not afraid," said Muppy, pushing her glasses up on her nose and taking her plate over to the sink. "But weather's here, all around us, and the other is, you know, sort of different."

Their mother sighed and poured herself more

11

iced tea. "How about raising the shades, Mup. The sun's almost down, and they block the air."

As Muppy did a handstand across the living room, their mother turned to Thad and said, "Don't tease her, please." And Thad noticed the little white lines that webbed around her eyes through her sunburn. Lines that hadn't been there other summers, that seemed to stand out and make her eyes dark and tired.

Muppy pulled up the outside shade, and Thad and his mother watched the red-orange sun sliding lower in the sky.

"It's still glarey," Ellen St. Clair said, getting up to clear the table. "But I hate that shade down; it gives everything such a closed-in feeling, like being in a box. I hate to be closed in, to feel like—"

She stopped abruptly, concentrating on scraping the plates into the trash can. From the back of the house came the gentle click of the curtain cords as they hit against the windows, caught in the breeze that came from the ocean.

And still the words "closed-in feeling" hung suspended in the early evening heat, and Thad and his mother seemed to avoid them and work around them as they did the dishes.

"Hey Mom," said Muppy, wiping off the table with one hand and holding the Grimm's tightly with the other, "tonight is *Rapunzel*. That's one of my favorites, but I had to wait till its turn came up. If

I get them out of order it won't work . . . about Daddy coming home I mean, when the stories are done—"

Thad kicked the plastic trash can out of the way. "It won't work anyway. I've told you that. You tell her, Mom. It won't work. It doesn't matter about the stories or whether you read *Rapoozle* in or out of order or whether you read it at all. It just doesn't matter."

But for once Muppy refused to be baited. She simply went on talking and dripping water from the sponge as she wiped off the counters, leaving watery swirls on the formica.

"Not *Rapoozle*—it's *Rapunzel,* after a vegetable, 'cause her mother wanted the witch's rampion and she gave it to her, and then she, the mother, had to give her the baby, who was named Rapunzel—I'm glad nobody named me Lettuce—and then the witch locked her up in this tower with no doors, and nobody could get in except the witch, and Rapunzel let down her hair and. . . ."

Muppy stopped in the middle of her sentence, with the words jumbling all around her. She stood with the sponge dripping water onto the floor and looked at her mother and brother. And in a suddenly small voice she asked, "Is Daddy locked up like that—in a tower without doors?"

From the outside came the roar of a powerboat as it picked up speed on leaving the inlet.

13

Muppy held up the book. "Maybe an extra story sometime would make the time go faster—till Daddy gets home. Maybe—"

"Oh, God," said Thad, slamming his fist against the front of the refrigerator. Ellen St. Clair put her hand on her son's arm. "Take the dog out, Thad. Go for a walk. You'll feel better, and before you know it, Peter'll be here."

Thad rooted for the leash in the drawer and headed downstairs to collect the dog from his post by the bayside door. As he went, he heard his mother talking quietly to Muppy. Words he knew she had already told her over and over.

"No, not in a tower, Muppy. Daddy's at Allenwood, the federal prison in Pennsylvania, you know that. And if the stories help to count the days, all well and good. But you know, we've told you before. . . ."

And Thad slid the screen door shut behind him and went around the side of the house to the street.

CHAPTER 2

Thad took the golden retriever and ran down Bayside Drive. He ran as hard as he could, driving the soles of his tennis shoes into the street so that the bottoms of his feet burned and stung. He ran past the cottages, gray and weathered; past the Captain's Cove Motel with its blinking lights and "No Vacancy" sign; past the empty lots and the town houses built out over the water on pilings. He ran down Bayside to the baseball diamond, then turned around and started back. He ran until the dog pulled against the leash and sat down abruptly in the middle of the street.

"OK, Barney, that's enough," said Thad, rubbing the dog's head. "Heat's got you, hasn't it? Come on." And together he and Barney stepped over the stubby remains of a fence and onto the narrow beach covered with stones and shells and upside-down horseshoe crabs and great tangled clumps of seaweed. He unhooked the leash and threw a stick, watching the big dog swim silently out into the water, his head gliding along the surface. The sun had set and the darkness settled in quickly around them both.

Thad stood for a few minutes listening to the cupping noises the dog made with his paws and the screech of birds from the island in the middle of the bay. Then he whistled for Barney, pulling him quickly back over the fence before he had a chance to roll on the beach.

"You smell bad enough without rolling in that mess. It's not fair that they don't let dogs up on the ocean beach in summer," said Thad, jumping back as Barney shook off the excess bay water. The dog threw himself down in the sand by the side of the road, rolling and stretching, arching his back and pawing at the air.

"Come on, Barney, cut it out." Thad tugged at the leash, heading up the wooden ramp to the old fishing pier. A fisherman packing his gear grunted at Thad, "Nothing doing here tonight. Storm's coming, though."

Thad stood for a minute listening to the man's footsteps echoing on the pier, then he sat down, leaning his back against a wooden post. Barney sniffed the fish smells on the pier then flopped down next to him.

From the two blocks away, out of the pocket of quiet that surrounded him, Thad heard the sound of traffic, the bleat of horns, as the cars crowded their way to the southern end of town, where the amusement rides and the casinos were. He knew that the boardwalk would be thronged with people, and for a minute he thought of taking Barney home then heading out looking for something to do. But he wasn't quite ready to go home.

He felt bad that he had screamed at Muppy, felt a funny burning place inside of himself that he alternately wanted to squash out and fan and cultivate so as to ache with its pain. His mother said it was from being fourteen. But Thad fought against that idea the way he fought against a lot of other things that summer.

Sometimes Thad fought so hard that he was bone tired. It was as though a terrible sticky exhaustion had taken hold of him, and sometimes, like tonight, he would have to run and pound his feet into the pavement to prove that he could still move—to prove that, unlike his father, he was free.

And then the thoughts that Thad had fought against came slamming down against him, and he crouched back against the post, pulling his knees up close to his chest. And he let the thoughts and memories beat and pull him, just as, as a child sitting

17

at the water's edge, he had let the waves gouge and wash around him and had tensed his body to keep from being sucked out into the undertow.

And he remembered, summers ago, leaning back against the strong, staunchly held legs of his father as he laughed down at him and said, "It's OK, Thad. The ocean's nothing to be afraid of so long as you watch the undertow."

Thad uncramped his legs and stretched them out in front of him. He looked up at the sky and heard the dog stir in his sleep beside him.

It had started in May when his father had gone to prison. But actually, Thad knew it had started earlier: in February, when the auditors had taken their report to the president of the savings and loan where his father had been an officer.

And the front page of the newspaper had seemed to fairly swell and clamor with news until it burst, leaving only a trace of minor stories on an inside page.

Thad shifted his position, grinding his back against the post so that the wood dug into his shoulder blades.

After the original explosion in the newspapers, Thad had thought that nothing could be worse. He had thought that things would gradually recede, like water seeping into the sand, leaving only a faint tracing on their lives.

But he had been wrong.

There had followed months of alternate silence and confusion; months when his father had been at home, drifting from room to room and window to window, dragging a shadow behind him like a tattered afghan; months when his father's overcoat had hung in the closet all day, his car parked at the curb like a sentinel. And Thad cringed to remember how he had devised ways to keep from bringing his own friends into the house, meeting them instead on streetcorners and by the vacant field. He remembered his mother's forced cheerfulness that stretched like taut rubber bands around them all; and Muppy, who dipped in and out of every day with her awareness just barely honed to what was going on; and Bridget, who unlike himself, seemed able to pull back away from it all.

And he remembered other things: the telephone that stayed strangely quiet; conversations that seemed to turn aside, eyes unmet; the dinnertimes that ached with unsaid words and the deafening clatter of knives and forks.

Thad's skin crawled as he remembered those unspoken conversations. He could taste again his own feeling of relief when his father had actually left in May for prison, and the taste was bitter. But bitterer still was the thought of going with his mother at the end of August to see his father . . . to visit him there—in that place, a word that Thad had never been able to say out loud.

"Prison," he tried to shout over the slap of the

19

water against the pier. But the word caught and choked him and came out a whisper. And everything inside of Thad drew back and shriveled.

A tourist boat went down the bay heading for the harbor at the end of town, and Thad caught the sound of laughter and singing. He watched the lights until the boat rounded a point of land, then he slid forward, the seat of his pants scratching against the sand on the pier, and sat with his legs dangling over the edge. Behind him the dog scuffled then inched forward, dropping his head in Thad's lap. Lightning faintly streaked the sky to the north.

The headboat, going up the bay every night after supper and coming back by dark, was one of the things that Thad thought of in his life as constant—just as Peter coming every summer was a constant, and the rise and fall of the tides, the way the moon rode lower in the summer sky.

They had always come to the beach for the summer, arriving early in June and staying until after Labor Day. A long, unbroken stretch of time, with his father coming on Friday nights and leaving on Monday mornings, only to come again on Friday. And the house in the city was another constant, somehow always there, sticking to his father's city clothes when he arrived for weekends bringing the mail and news from town. And on those weekends, in those other summers, the house at the beach had come strangely, vibrantly alive.

Thad listened to the sound of the bell buoy and thought of the house in town, suddenly far away.

The house was occupied this summer . . . sublet . . . filled with another family: an English family wanting a house in the States to use as a vacation headquarters. It was a family his mother had heard about, friends of a friend. His mother had seen it as a way to make extra money, the way she had seen her job in the hotel coffee shop, while still keeping as much as possible to the way things had always been.

Thad thought about the other family living in his house; of another someone in his bed, and other toothbrushes over the sink. And he suddenly remembered one time years ago, when Muppy was small, when they hadn't come to the beach for the entire summer; when the house had, in fact, been rented to someone else for June and July. And when they had finally come on August 1, the house still had the vibrations and impressions of the other tenants. There had been a strange blue bedroom slipper under the couch, and rings from coffee cups on the tabletops, and the wrong kind of soap in the bathroom that his mother had quickly disposed of, talking all the while about not liking to waste, but. . . . And to Thad it had been as though their whole family had been blotted out and they had to very carefully reinstate themselves, day by day.

And he wondered if that was happening in the

21

city, wondered if when they went home they would have to go about putting their selfness back into the house. And his wondering gave way to a kind of excitement that left him sweaty under the arms as he thought of them going home after Labor Day, his mother and the girls and him, and pressing themselves, like iron-on patches, back onto the house. The excitement grew and churned inside of him as he thought how it would be just the four of them putting themselves back, replacing the other family, filling up the places they had left. Just the four of them, and not his father who would still be in prison: who wouldn't be there, wouldn't displace any emptiness or make any impression.

And the excitement caught Thad and he half-rose and reached for a sentence from his childhood: "And they lived happily ever after."

A couple came up behind Thad on the pier, holding onto one another, scuffling and tugging and giggling at one another. Thad wanted to turn around and not turn around all at once. Lightning forked the sky, and the girl screamed and there was the sound of scuffling again, and then they were quiet.

Thad dropped back onto the pier. "It's a fairy tale, damn it. 'Happily ever after' is a fairy tale— like Muppy and her stories. He'll come back wherever we are. They only gave him a year and with parole and all. . . . Any time after six months, they said."

22

The boats came one after another, and Thad checked his watch, knowing it must be ten after the hour and that the drawbridge was open. He peered through the encroaching dark, noting the marlin and tuna flags that flew from the outriggers, mentally cataloging the names of the boats and their places in the marina. He saw the *White Witch,* the *Lucky Day,* the *Neptune,* and the *Kitty Hawk.* He saw the *Genevieve* and the *Water Works.*

He was looking for the *Sea Hunter.*

The wake slogged against the bulkhead, and Thad felt the pier sway beneath him. The wind picked up sharply and there was a distant rumble of thunder. The dog whimpered, pushing closer to Thad. The couple in back of him scrambled up, and Thad heard them running, felt their footsteps on the pier.

The boat loomed up out of nowhere, churning along in the wake of the boats coming in from a day's fishing. Thad saw the red and green running lights, made out the familiar white lines of the *Sea Hunter* etched against the dark. He saw Peter standing on the bow, braced against the wind like a modern-day Columbus, in a yellow slicker. And then the boat was past, and Thad heard the squawk of the bullhorn as Mr. Hunter called to the harbormaster.

Thad knew that any other year he would have raced down the road, around the end of the inlet,

23

taking great gulping breaths and pushing himself onward, trying to be there when the *Sea Hunter* docked, standing ready to catch the lines when Peter threw them.

The dark inched closer around him, and Thad abandoned himself to it, watching the lightning as it patterned the sky. Slowly, reluctantly, he stood up, reaching for the leash. "Come on, Barney, let's go home. It's raining."

Inside the house the lights blinked in the storm. His mother was at the table writing a letter, and Muppy was crouched down into one end of the couch with her hands over her ears.

Thad stood in the middle of the living room floor and let the water run off him. He dug in the pocket of his shorts and pulled out a gumball, slightly lint covered.

"Here Muppy," he called over the sound of the storm, and tossed her the gum. "Don't say I never gave you anything."

His mother looked at him over the top of her glasses. "Oh Thad, Peter was here. He said to come over. He's waiting for you."

CHAPTER 3

Thad sat at the breakfast table and looked across the living room and through the sliding doors that spanned the front of the room. The *Sea Hunter,* moored in the slip directly across the inlet, seemed to be framed by the St. Clair's front porch.

He saw Peter come up out of the cabin and jump onto the land, saw him start up the road that ran behind the marina, his red hair glinting in the morning sun. Thad watched until Peter disappeared behind the clubhouse, then began a kind of mental countdown measuring how long it would take him to go around the end of the inlet, along behind the motel and down the street past the cottages and the church and zigzag back towards the bay again. In other years the boys had speculated about a bridge or a ramp running back and forth, had planned elaborate high-wire engineering feats. They had, at times, resorted to surf mats and homemade rafts to cover the one hundred feet of water between boat and house.

"Thank heavens the sun's out," said Bridget St. Clair, pulling a tee shirt over her yellow bathing suit and sitting down at the table. "Today's my day off and T.J. and I are going sailing."

"It rained last night," said Muppy. "Did you hear it? And the tide was so high it looked like it was going to come up over the dock."

"Hear it?" Bridget lifted the corner of Thad's sports page out of the milk pitcher and reached for the orange juice. "I was in it. After work we went to 78th Street. There was supposed to be a beach party, but instead about nine hundred of us were squished into this little apartment."

"You could do something with us today, me and Thad," said Muppy, licking strawberry jelly off her thumb. "We could go crabbing with chicken necks and the net and—"

"Crabs? Don't talk to me about crabs. I work in a crab house, remember?" Bridget caught her long blond hair in a twist and pinned it on top of her head. "Boy, it's hot already. Maybe next year I'll be something else, and not a waitress. Last night I had this table . . . a fifty-dollar check and they left me eighty cents and two hard crabs. Very funny."

Thad brushed his sisters' conversation away like a mosquito. He heard Peter's voice outside on the street. "Hi, great. We got in last night before the storm. OK, see you." He heard the click of the gate and the slide of the downstairs door. "Hi, Barney old boy. How're you doing?" He heard the two-at-a-time footsteps on the stairs—and Peter was there, flopping into a chair and reaching for a doughnut.

"Hey, where were you last night? I was dying for a pizza with everything—waited and waited. Then I must have zonked out 'cause next thing I knew it was tomorrow—today. Let's get going. We've got places to go, things to check out. Want to see what's new at the casino. And, hey, guess what? We might have a job, both of us. Mr. Fredericks who owns the *Kitty Hawk* needs a crew, and my dad says we might get it. The marlin tournament's coming up. Have to look for him, maybe at the beach."

"Hi, Peter," said Bridget. "Thad's got a job, taking care of Muppy, now that Mom's working, now that—"

Thad jumped up, folding the newspaper and rattling cereal boxes. "You could watch her today," he said to Bridget. Suddenly, as much as he had wanted Peter not to come, he wanted to be off with him, going places and checking on things. "It wouldn't kill you, just today."

"Well, she's your job, Mom said in the beginning of the summer. And anyway, it's not as though

27

she needs watching, not like she's three or something."

"She's the cat. That's what Mom says. And besides I'm not anybody's job. I'm just me," said Muppy heading for the television.

"Yes you are, you're Thad's. Like the breakfast dishes are yours. Everybody has to help."

Muppy flipped the dial on the TV until she got the local time-and-weather station. *"Can* we go crabbing, Thad, and Peter too? The weather's OK. Tru-weather says—"

"Someday, but not today. I told the guys at the beach I'd help them with their beach stand. They're counting on me, besides—"

"Are not," said Muppy. "They just let you hang around there so they can go eat. And you think you're so cool. Like you had a job or something."

"Well I would have a job except I'm stuck watching you." Thad picked his cereal bowl up off the table and drank the milk out of the bottom.

Bridget turned from the sink. "Thad, that's disgusting. Stop slurping and put that bowl down. Anyway, Mom said you had to help, and Dad too . . . he wrote—"

Thad dropped the bowl into the sink with a loud clatter. "No wonder those people left you two crabs. It suits your personality. Besides, Mom said before she left for work that you should put a load of wash in. Remember, everybody has to help."

"Crimeny. You could have told me. I'm going to be late."

"Hey Bridget," said Muppy, "last night was *Rapunzel*. I'm up to that already." But her sister was heading down the stairs to the washing machine. "Peter, did you ever read *Rapunzel?* I have this book and—"

"Come on," said Thad, turning the water on full force. "Let's clean up here."

"Yeah," said Peter taking the last doughnut out of the box. "Muppy can come with us, but hurry up, you guys. The sun's out."

Thad walked the three blocks between the bay and the ocean as though he were alone. The day was already hot, the sky sharp and blue after last night's storm. And already, in the streets, little tucks of tar were turning soft and liquid. Peter swung on ahead, crisscrossing the street, jumping up and swatting at stop signs, leaping over porch steps and fire hydrants. Thad heard the scuff of Muppy's flip-flops behind him like a whisper. But he didn't wait. He knew that Muppy would catch up, would find him no matter where he went.

Thad followed Peter up the ramp and onto the boardwalk, dodging children in strollers and the up-and-down procession of walkers. "Hey," said Peter, draping his towel around his neck, "I'm going to check out the casino for a while, then look for Mr.

Fredericks about the job on the boat. Maybe he'll let you go anyway, let you bring Muppy along. She's an OK kid."

"I don't know." Thad rubbed his foot across the worn wood of the boardwalk. "I don't think my mom . . . I guess I better—"

"Where is she, anyway, your mother, I mean?"

"At the Beach House. She got a job as a cashier. Said it was boring, sort of, all day at the beach and stuff."

"Well, I'll be back in a minute." Peter disappeared into the crowd.

Thad stood for a moment, glad that Peter had gone, wishing he had gone with him. He jumped off the steps and onto the glaring sand that burned the bottoms of his feet. Swallowing back the sudden wince of pain, he wandered over to the beach stand. Music from a transistor radio blared and circled outward, touching the edges of music from other radios on nearby towels. A pile of green and yellow surf mats lay next to stacked up chaises and beach umbrellas, and in the center two boys were sprawled in sand chairs. Thad stood for a moment looking down at the boys, older and oiled against the sun. He looked across the beach, past the orange lifeguard stand to the ocean.

One of the boys opened his eyes and blinked. "Oh hi, Thad. Thought you were a customer. Sit down. Take a load off your feet. Hey Pat, Thad's here. Want to go eat? Me, I'm starved."

30

Pat sat up, reaching for a shirt all in one motion. "Yeah, OK. Hi, Thad. We were hoping you'd come by. Here, take my watch." He tossed Thad the watch and the lined pad with the rentals in it. "Come on, Bill. Let's eat."

Thad sat for a minute watching the boys as they stopped first to talk to a crowd of girls, then made their way up onto the boardwalk. He strapped on the watch and peeled off his shirt. Reaching for the radio, he twirled the dials, adjusting the antenna. Then very deliberately he pushed one chair out of the way and turned the other to face the sun. Helping himself to Bill's Ocean Gold, he rubbed the oil liberally over his arms and chest. Then he settled back.

There was a sudden thud next to him, and Thad felt himself splattered with sand as Muppy said, "Hi, Thad, I'm back. What'll we do? I found Jenny over there, down by the water with her mother. After a while we're gonna get ice cream. You want to hold my money, but I know exactly how much I have."

Thad tried to swat the oily sand off his arms, but succeeded only in grinding it into his skin. "For Pete's sake Muppy, get lost. Go play with Jenny. Here, I'll let you use one of the surf mats, but you've got to promise not to go out too far, and to come when I say it's time. Now go, and don't drag that mat in the sand. I've got a stand to run."

Thad was just settling back again when a just-in-from-the-city man came inquiring about an um-

31

brella. And Thad didn't know there could be so many questions about one umbrella. Fussy, nit-picking questions: are they sturdy and what about the wind, and who puts them up and takes them down and. . . . Finally, still looking doubtfully at the rows of umbrellas lining the water's edge, he gave Thad his name and money and beckoned to his wife. Throwing the umbrella over his shoulder, Thad marched across the beach, with the man and his wife following close behind him. He chose an empty space close to the shore, and for a minute Thad stood poised. He thought of the way Pat and Bill drove the pointed ends of the sticks into the sand, swiftly and surely, so that the umbrellas stood straight and unmoving. The smooth wooden pole felt clumsy in his hand and for a moment Thad had visions of having to pound and struggle to get the umbrella into the sand, where it would surely tilt and sway and, with the slightest breeze, career crazily across the beach.

Thad licked his upper lip, tasting the thickness of zinc oxide. He drew his arm back and shot the stick forward, slanting it at just the right angle, straightening it sharply, snapping open the top. And the umbrella stood straight and tall, its edges whipping slightly in the breeze.

As he walked back to the beach stand, he hummed a jagged tune and he turned slightly on the balls of his feet with every step.

Thad studied the people around him on the beach: the fish-belly white skin of those just in from the city, the screeching red sunburn of those trying to wedge a summer into several days, and the deep, steady tan of the all-summer residents. He looked quickly down at his own arm, measuring the tan. The sound of laughter swung around him, and he grabbed for a magazine, burying his face.

Over close to the steps three almost teen-age girls were struggling to flatten a large white bedspread on the sand. They giggled, flopping down on edges and catching other edges with their hands and feet and bottles of baby oil. Thad looked over the top of his magazine as the girls turned and stretched, smearing themselves with oil and brushing sand off the spread.

That's one eight and two sevens on a scale of one to ten, thought Thad. Or maybe two eights and a nine, as the girl in the middle undid the straps of her bathing suit, tucking them down in front. He reconsidered their ages, deciding they might be fourteen, maybe the one in the middle a little older. He had the strange feeling that the girls were looking at him, were deliberately making their voices louder than they had to be. He felt his face go red and burning, and when one of the girls started toward him smiling broadly, he looked quickly over his shoulder, to make sure she wasn't looking at someone behind him, before he smiled back.

"Hi. You know what time it is?" she asked.

"Uh, sure. It's one o'clock," said Thad, trying to drag the words out into a conversation. "One o'clock and thirty-seven seconds."

"Thanks a lot," the girl answered, and he could hear her friends giggling across the way. "Nice beach stand you got. See you later." And Thad watched as she walked back to her friends, watched the way her backside twitched with every step, watched as she turned and waved back at him and together the three girls walked down to the water.

Yeah, thought Thad, two eights and a nine. And a nine's the best you can hope for.

He followed the girls with his eyes as they walked along the shore till they blended in with the crowd, then let his eyes skim out over the water. He studied the waves, watching their thrust, the arch of the breakers, sizing them up for surfing. Thad's concentration seemed to blot out the everyday scene, filtering out the people and flattening umbrellas until in his mind he saw the beach the way it was after five-thirty, when the surfers were allowed to take over. Last summer Thad had begun to think that he was really getting a hold on surfing, though he had still wiped out more often than not. But somehow, this year the surfboard had stayed emptily in the corner of his bedroom and the yellow wax was still molded over the windowsill where it had melted in a succession of afternoon suns, and he had never bothered to scrape it off. But now, in one of those sudden pockets of stillness that come at the beach, he heard only the sound of the waves. He felt his legs braced, his feet apart on the board, felt the lift of the wave beneath him as. . . .

"I found him," said Peter, flopping onto the sand and wriggling his back to make a hollowed out place for himself. "Mr. Fredericks, I mean, and he's going to take me on . . . to crew, and help him get ready and stuff, and cleaning the boat afterwards. Would've taken you too but I told him. . . . Asked me to find somebody else. Who's in town? Tommy, or any of the Bradys? I've got to meet him back at the boat in a while . . . to learn the ropes and all."

For a few minutes the boys were quiet, listening to the sound of the surf and the bleat of the lifeguard's whistle.

A man went by carrying a surf mat on his head and followed by a string of little children.

"Hey," said Peter, propping himself up on his elbows, "remember all the times when we were little and your father brought us to the beach, mostly when my dad was off fishing? Remember how he taught us to ride the waves? And how about the first time he took us on the surf mat and you wiped out?" Peter laughed out loud, making frog noises in his throat and waving his arms. "Remember how you. . . ."

And Thad remembered. He remembered that first ride and the way a giant wave had flipped the mat over on top of him. He could taste again the grit of sand between his teeth; he felt his fingers clawing the shore, felt the weight of canvas and the terrible pushing out of breath. And in one quick motion, his father had lifted mat and boy into the air and together they had headed out to meet another wave.

"And remember the sand castles," said Peter, rolling onto his stomach and digging his hands into the sand. "How we'd make the roads and windows and stuff. It was kind of neat, your father making all those turrets and battlements and all. . . ."

In his mind Thad saw his father still kneeling by the water's edge, piling, carving, wedging the sand, long after he and Peter had wandered off looking for something else to do.

He remembered other things, the walks early in the morning and late at night. He remembered so much: flying kites and hunting shells, watching the sea gulls soar, and the way his father had taught him to listen to the conch shell.

And he hurt with the remembering. He hurt with the way he used to feel. A wild, racing, leaping kind of feeling that he had ridden like the crest of a wave.

He thought of Muppy and her constant talk of their father coming home.

36

And he hurt for the way Muppy still could feel.

Peter jumped up. "I've got to go. Have to meet Mr. Fredericks back on his boat. About the job. See you."

The silence was broken then. The memories splintered as Bill and Pat came back, dropping onto the sand and reaching for the radio, rearranging the chairs.

"Thanks, Thad, for letting us get away." And they turned to talk to the girls who were with them.

Thad inched over on the beach, not sure whether to go or stay. He felt at once displaced and in the way. The beach stand was no longer his. The radio blared. The girls laughed.

Ought to have my own job, he thought, pushing his feet out into the sand. A real job.

The lifeguard blew his whistle, and Thad suddenly remembered Muppy. He stood up slowly and moved down to the water to check on her.

CHAPTER 4

The devil's beating his wife, thought Thad, remembering his grandmother's old saying as he watched the sun filtering through the steadily falling rain. And almost before the thought was out, the sky lowered and the rain intensified, slanting against the library window.

It had been like that all morning—changing patterns of dark and light, murky patches of gray broken by a sudden burst of sunlight that made the puddles steam and the sidewalk begin to dry in mottled designs, and then another onslaught of rain. It seemed to Thad that he had spent the morning opening and closing windows, and mopping window sills when he had closed them too late.

Once, when Peter had stopped by during a

longer-than-usual sunny spell, Thad had tried to drag Muppy off to the beach, even going so far as to promise her a hot dog and an Italian ice. But Muppy had dug herself in, staying firmly planted in front of the television set and its steady drone of "intermittent shower activity" and "weather patterns." After lunch the rain had stopped and the sky had lightened around the edges and Thad had hurried Muppy along to the library. He planned to leave her there for the movies and story hour and then head up to the boardwalk looking for something to do, even if the something involved nothing more than watching the ocean.

But no sooner had they gotten to the door of the library than the rain had begun again; and the winds, that gusted and flattened the spindly grass outside. Muppy had grabbed hold of Thad, the water from their slickers running in rivulets onto the library floor.

"Promise me you'll stay, Thad, and you won't go off. Right there, in those chairs, so I'll know you're here. Unless . . ." She blinked at him through water-streaked glasses. "Unless you want to watch the movie too. It's *The Red Balloon*. . . ."

A really weird kid, thought Thad, slouching down in his chair and flipping the pages of *Sports Illustrated*. She'll do anything, isn't afraid of anything—the ocean, the Wild Mouse, the top of the Ferris wheel, as long as the weather's OK. And suddenly he thought of a song he often heard Bridget singing at home, mostly in the shower when she was rushing to go out. "Don't rain on my parade," went the words. That was all he knew—no verses, nothing else . . . just "Don't rain on my parade." And what, he wondered as he settled into a lacrosse story, had ever rained on Muppy's parade?

The library smelled of slickers and canvas tennis shoes. There was a general hum of voices and scraping of chairs and the sort of swooshing sound the door made when it opened and closed. And superimposed on it all was the beat of rain on the flat roof above. The tables were crowded, and the corner where the mysteries were kept was three deep as people traded books and conversation. A woman with a leathery tan and tightly curled gray hair settled into the chair next to Thad, dropping her raincoat and a grocery bag and a canvas tote bag full of books on the floor between them. She glared at Thad, as though thinking that if his feet already weren't a size eleven she would have the room she deserved.

Pushing lower in his seat, Thad tried to concentrate on what he was reading. He wished the librarian would tell everybody to keep quiet, but he didn't think librarians told grownups to be quiet very often. A toddler dragged a squawking wooden duck across the floor, and from the meeting room next door came the sound of music from Muppy's movie. The woman next to Thad folded the newspaper with great crackling sounds and leaned across him to put it on the table. Then she yoo-hooed and waved frantically to a friend across the room.

Thad turned sideways in his chair and stuffed a finger in one ear, forcing himself back into the lacrosse story. And for a while he was lost in it, feeling the thwack of the ball as it hit the pocket, the snug weight of the helmet on his head.

But gradually, almost insidiously, words reached in and poked at him. Thad pushed them back, concentrating on his magazine, determined to win out over the tote bag woman next to him and her friend who had somehow nudged in beside her. Words swarmed like gnats around him as the two women warmed to their subject. And Thad brushed his hand in front of his face, trying to swat away "Can you imagine . . . saw her myself . . . today . . . they say. . . ."

"Well, all I can say," said the woman next to him as she rearranged herself in the chair and lit a cigarette, dragging the ashtray closer, over Thad's offending feet, "all I can say is she certainly has stood by him. Ellen St. Clair has. . . ."

And Thad felt a thousand arrows digging into him, felt his already rain-damp clothes turn wet with sweat. He saw his hands shake, and he doubled over as something seemed to gouge and twist inside his stomach.

All around him the words pulsed on.

41

"Working as a cashier at the Beach House. Saw her there myself."

"Not surprised, though I don't guess they can pay much back that way; embezzlement you know. . . ."

"His mother—fine family you know. Father was a judge . . . grandson of a governor. The St. Clair name. . . ."

"And what on earth kind of a job will Thadeus St. Clair be able to get after this. Now I ask you, and do you think Ellen St. Clair. . . ?"

And again Thad heard his mother's name stretched out across the library.

He burned with humiliation, but it was cross-hatched with a kind of fascination so that he was physically unable to move. He wanted to hear; and he wanted not to hear.

He wanted to tell the woman next to him, and her friend with the blathering ways, to shut up. He wanted to yell the words, but he couldn't even say them as he ground his hand into a fist and pushed it into the vinyl seat cushion.

"Yes," the voice next to Thad went on, "it's amazing the way she stuck by him. Not many wives in this day and age would. . . ."

"And more than his own mother did, they say. . . ."

"Why, do you know she even took those chil-

42

dren into court, the day he was sentenced. The older two, I guess. Even Ellen St. Clair wouldn't have taken that little one. . . ."

"A girl and a boy. You're right, what I heard . . . wanted them there with their father. Right out in the open for all to see. I heard. . . ."

"Well you heard wrong," something inside of Thad screamed back. But he could tell by the way the women chittered on that he had not spoken out loud. And still the silent screams went on. "You're wrong. Dead wrong. Both of you. She took Bridget, and not me 'cause I threw up. Vomited right there in the front hall on the Oriental rug. Mom and Bridget went off to court to stand by him and I stayed home. And the thing about it was that I was glad. Really, really glad."

And Thad's head seemed to swell and burst with the unsaid words.

He saw Muppy coming towards him, mouth open to speak, to call his name. And Thad knew he had to keep her quiet. He waved to her, and called, "Hi kid, how was the movie? Good I bet. Here, how about putting this magazine away for me, over there. And we can go. And guess what? It's stopped raining; sun's out, to stay I bet." Thad tossed her the *Sports Illustrated* and jumped up, lurching slightly.

The woman next to him moved over into his chair, rearranging her belongings. She glowered up at Thad. "Young man, you had best learn to keep quiet in the library. People are trying to read, you know."

Muppy stuffed her slicker under her arm and slogged through the puddles, making a trail of wet footprints on the already dry street. Thad trailed behind her, half hearing her account of the movie, half hearing the strident voice of the woman in the library.

"Hey Thad, you're not listening," said Muppy, circling back to talk to him. "Know what I'm going to do? I'm going to Jenny's, OK? Here, you take my raincoat, will you? And thanks for taking me. See you." And Thad watched as she disappeared around the corner.

Thad sat cross-legged on the dock and lifted his face up to the sun. His jeans made him feel hot and steamy, but he didn't want to go in and change. He didn't want to upset the precarious balance of thoughts he had carried home from the library, holding them carefully like so many building blocks.

A gull cried overhead, and Thad opened his eyes watching the bird drop down into the water, seeing it as a silhouette against the glaring sunlight. He flattened his hands on the dock in front of him, bending his fingers back until they hurt, as if physical pain could take away the feeling deep inside of him.

"Ellen St. Clair certainly has stood by him."

And Thad laid the words out on the dock in front of him, gouging and prying them away from the woman's awful voice as one would prod a barnacle from a piling. He scraped and filed at them until he made the words his own.

"She, Mom, she certainly has stood by him."

It—this standing by—was something Thad had wondered about almost as much as he wondered about why his father had done what he had done.

Not so much a why, really, as a how. How had she stood by him? How had his mother done it, through the long tortured months at home before the re-arraignment, when his father had pleaded guilty? Then there were the extra weeks before his father had gone back to court for the sentencing, with his mother and Bridget dragging themselves along while he had stayed home and vomited on the rug— the cardboard weeks and months when they had all marched through every day like Muppy's paper dolls. And even in that cardboard world his mother had been the only real thing, the only flesh and blood person doing flesh and blood things: cleaning the house and potting a plant; laughing, talking, crying, and calling them for dinner.

And something warm stirred inside of him. He remembered a night, between the charges and the final sentencing, a night when he had gone down late to get a glass of milk. He had come back past his parents' bedroom, and in that silent house, marked only by the tick of the grandfather clock, he had heard the sounds: the creak of his parents' bed, a kind of thrashing; a laugh, a sigh. And Thad had stood in the shadowed hall and the tracings of milk inside his mouth had turned sour.

The next morning when his mother came down to the kitchen, Thad was already there, smearing peanut butter and jelly onto bread and stuffing the sandwiches into a bag, leaving an hour early for school, never looking her in the face.

The gull cried again, dipping back into the water, worrying at a dead fish. Thad felt the sweat run down his back, felt his legs cramped beneath him.

He heard the metal clank of the mailbox, and his mother came around the side of the house carrying the mail. And suddenly he felt as though he were back in the kitchen on that morning several months ago, had the same feeling of wanting to hurry off, of not wanting to look his mother in the eye, as if she could see inside his head.

Ellen St. Clair sat down on the wooden step, holding the letters up against her cheek. "Hi Thad. How was your day? Where's Muppy?"

"Off somewhere with Jenny." He stretched his legs out in front of him and lay back on the dock, closing his eyes.

46

"Here's a letter for her, and one for you too . . . from your father."

Thad felt his mother put the envelope on his chest. He heard her stand up.

"I'm going in now and get a shower. It's hot out here." He heard the screen door slide open. "Oh, and Thad . . ." she paused. "You will try and answer this one, won't you? It would mean so much."

And Thad waited until he was sure his mother was well inside before he took the letter and shoved it underneath a bottle of baby oil by the side of the door. He watched for a moment while the oil from the bottle spread and settled into the white of the envelope.

CHAPTER 5

"I'm gonna have blueberry waffles with whipped cream," said Muppy, coming around the side of the house with Barney on the leash. She stopped to watch Thad hang a pair of trunks and a slightly gray beach towel on the line.

"Unless I have French toast, except we do get that at home. How about you? You been to the beach already, Thad?"

Thad turned and followed Muppy into the house, unhooking the leash and rumpling the big dog's coat. "No, that's from the day before yesterday. Forgot to take it out. What do you mean, blueberry waffles?"

"Mom's note. Didn't you see it? On the table upstairs. She said we could come to the Beach House

48

for breakfast, today, right now. And I'm getting blueberry waffles unless I get—"

"Who's talking about waffles?" called a sleepy voice, as Bridget appeared at the door of her bedroom.

"Me, I am. Mom said we could come for breakfast and get whatever we want and I want—"

"Oh yum," said Bridget. "Treats. Hey you guys, wait for me. I just have to wash my hair and take a shower."

"Oh come on, Bridget," said Thad, "that'll take hours and I'm starved. You don't have to wash your hair—just come."

"Sure I do; it's filthy, and besides there's this guy I know, he's a busboy at the Beach House and you never know. I'll just be a minute."

"I know your minutes—more like hours. I'm getting a bowl of cereal so I can make it up there."

They walked up the steps like three ducks in a row, Thad heading for the kitchen, and Bridget with her shampoo and creme rinse, on her way to the shower, and Muppy, walking carefully, arms held out, balancing the book of *Grimm's* on her head.

"Hurry up, Bridget, we're starving," said Muppy, pushing the words out smoothly so as not to topple the book from her head. "You could take your shower downstairs and save time."

49

"Save time? Two seconds to come up the steps, and besides the downstairs bathroom is scuzzy, from you and Thad using it and—"

"You live there too," said Thad. "You could clean it and—"

But his words were lost as Bridget slammed the bathroom door and turned the shower on full force.

"You know what, Thad?" said Muppy, sitting down carefully at the table with the book still on her head. "You know what? I read my story for today already, read it this morning 'cause I woke up early and I think I like that better because now we're one day closer to when Daddy gets home and the day's not even half gone. A trick, sort of. And you know what I read today? *The King of the Golden Mountain.* About this guy, a merchant, who didn't have any more money, and he met this dwarf, and the dwarf said he would give him some money if the merchant would give him the first thing that brushed against his leg when he got home, and the merchant said OK cause he thought it would be the dog, except it was his little son and so. . . ." Muppy tilted her head and let the book slide off into her hands. "You know what, Thad? Wouldn't it be neat? I mean Daddy needs money, and if somebody magic could give it to him I would do it, go with the dwarf I mean, 'cause it worked out OK in the end 'cause when the little boy grew up he got to be King of the Golden Mountain."

Thad spooned the pieces of banana out of his cereal, sliding them into his mouth one at a time, clamping his lips tight around them until they mushed together inside his mouth. He stared down at the sludge of sugar in the bottom of the bowl, scraping at it with his spoon, pushing the soggy Rice Krispies into it, blotting out Muppy's conversation, willing himself not to answer her.

From the bathroom came the sound of Bridget singing and the rush of water.

Muppy jumped up. "I'm going outside on the dock. Don't go without me." And she was gone, down the steps and out onto the dock, running to the end of the pier.

Thad went out onto the porch. He looked across at the marina, at the boats tied snugly to their moorings. Although the day was clear, an early morning wind had kept the fishermen from going out. Across from him the *Sea Hunter* rocked gently back and forth; he could see Mrs. Hunter cleaning the cabin windows. He wondered where Peter was.

Since Peter had come back, he and Thad had slipped into their pattern of every summer. But it was an uneasy kind of familiarity with Thad always on guard, careful to slide around the edges of conversations, to stay always on the surface of things.

Down below him Muppy sat on the piling at the end of the pier, swinging her legs, her hair, in the breeze, ruffing around her head.

51

Thad leaned on the railing, letting the wood dig into his arms, watching Muppy, who seemed to have forgotten about being the King of the Golden Mountain and going with the dwarf. She seemed to have forgotten everything as she waved to Mrs. Hunter across the way.

And Thad was left with the shadows of her conversation as it hung around him like the fadeout on a television set. He turned and went back inside, pouring another bowl of cereal, slicing another banana, waiting for Bridget, who still sang and sloshed away in the water in the bathroom.

When Bridget turned off the shower, the silence was startling. Things seemed to roar out at Thad: the sound of voices drifting in from outside; conversations skimming across the water as though they were next to him; the thud of a ball as Muppy threw it up against the side of the house, threw it and caught it and threw it again.

"I'm almost ready," called Bridget, opening the bathroom door and coming out swathed in a towel, with another wound around her head. "Don't leave without me." And she disappeared into her mother's room. "Hey Thad, call Muppy," she yelled over the sound of the blow dryer.

Thad sat waiting for his sisters and wishing he were doing something else. He felt like a hermit crab, the kind they sold up on the boardwalk, scuttling around, sideways and back and forth, living

52

in someone else's shell, never really venturing out on its own.

Thad caught a glimpse of the pushed-back thoughts that lined around him like the mirrors in the casino. And suddenly the thought glared out at him, reflecting back: convex and concave. Lumpy, sliding, twisting thoughts that pushed and pulled and gave him back himself in a series of pictures. He saw himself lying on the bottom bunk in his room staring up at the underneath side of the other bed, at the flattened coils of springs and the rumpled edges of sheet. He heard again the record as it throbbed and repeated itself until he grew to hate the very sound of the music, but still he allowed it to play over and over. He saw himself clumping along after Muppy, watching her far more than she needed watching. And then the pictures dwindled off, turning in on themselves emptily. Emptily. And he thought how his life this summer was as un-used as the surfboard that leaned in the corner of his room.

The ball hitting against the side of the house pulled him back. He heard Bridget talking from the back room and wondered if she had been talking to him. He got up slowly, gathering together a deep breath, ready to call Muppy in to go, to hurry Bridget along.

And suddenly Muppy was there, standing in front of him as though she had appeared like a genie from a lamp. In one hand she held a slippery plastic bottle of baby oil, and in the other a wilted envelope that flopped over as she handed it to him.

"Thad-e-us. You forgot. You didn't even open it. Your letter from Daddy, and I found it outside under the baby oil all crunkled up. Open it now. Can I read it? What does it say?"

Thad held the envelope and felt its limp dampness all the way through. His father's writing, that yesterday had seemed bold and threatening, now looked soft and somehow muzzy. He had forgotten the letter, had meant to shove it down into the garbage can, slipping it into the sliminess of cantaloupe rinds and coffee grounds without even opening it.

And now, here was the letter, back again, insistent, waiting to be opened while Muppy danced in circles around him saying, "Open it, Thad, open it," and Bridget stood by the door saying, "You all come on. I'm starved."

"No, wait," said Muppy, climbing up onto the kitchen counter and rooting in an old saltwater taffy box on top of the cabinets. "Here's my yesterday's letter so we can compare. Go ahead and read yours, Thad, because Mom says letters should be private unless people want them not to be and THEN you can let me read it."

Thad turned his back to Muppy, rustling the sheets of paper, trying to make letter-reading noises. But suddenly she was in front of him, her dark-

54

framed glasses seeming to grow and peer up at him from all directions.

"You're not reading. I can tell. And that's mean. When somebody takes the trouble to write to you, you could read it. Poor Daddy has. . . ."

Thad forced his eyes down on the page, trying to hold the written words back, the way he had tried to hold back the ocean when he was a child. And his eyes strained inside his head.

"Dear Son, Your mother tells me. . . ." (Don't call me that, screamed everything inside of Thad. Dear Son . . . no son . . . never son . . . never. . . .)

And Muppy slipped and slid around him, her bare feet whispering against the floor as she read, "Dear Muppy-wup, How's my girl? I was really glad to get your letter and the postcard of the beach, Wish I were there with you and your friend Jenny. Have you made any sand castles lately? . . ."

And Muppy's letter superimposed itself on the words he was trying not to read. By reading her own letter out loud, it seemed to Thad that she brought their father right into the room with them. The underneath part of his jaws ached as Muppy's voice raced on, as he heard her holding on to their father in a way Thad no longer could.

"Your mother tells me that you are a real help, watching Muppy for her. . . ." (Some help, thought Thad, slowing the words that leaped up at him. If I had a job, a paying job, not stuck here, not. . . .)

"And guess what, Muppy, I've been doing crafts. Can you imagine your old father actually making a birdhouse out of. . . ."

Something split inside of Thad. He heard the excitement in Muppy's voice and he wanted to take hold of that excitement and bundle it around her like a cocoon, stuffing it and wedging it around her to keep her safe. And at the same time his fingers itched to tear the cocoon away, to flatten out her voice and her thoughts until she saw things the way Thad knew them to be.

"And remember, Son. I'm counting on you to help your mother, take care of the house. . . ."

". . . birdhouse home to you as soon as I can. . . ." Muppy's voice rose and peaked. "Did you hear that, Thad? Daddy's made a birdhouse, and he's going to bring it home for me. He made it himself and—"

"A birdhouse? A lousy, rotten birdhouse? He made a. . . ." Thad heard the words pulling away from him, pulling so that he couldn't get them back, couldn't keep them from spiraling on without him. And while his words beat and swirled around him, he saw Muppy's face begin to crumple, to dissolve around the edges, growing smaller and smaller.

Thad heard his words race on. Loud, ugly, spitting words: "For him. That birdhouse is for him because he's a jailbird. A jailbird. A crook. Your father is a crook. Not a father like other people's;

56

like we're not like other people. And I've had it. I'm sick of it the way people talk and you thinking it's all OK like a birdhouse is OK. Something great. When all the time it's . . . and me taking care of you when I could have a job . . . and. . . ."

The words twisted up and spent themselves. And Thad saw Muppy's face grow smaller still, saw Bridget, standing by the kitchen table with her mouth open. He saw, as he turned towards the steps, Bridget folding her arms around Muppy.

He heard a sound, a cry, half choked, that rose up around them as he started down the steps. And he didn't know from which one of them it came.

CHAPTER 6

Thad went out the door and around the side of the house and bumped smack into Peter.

"Where're you going?"

"Out."

"Out where?"

"Nowhere. Anywhere. Everywhere." Thad started up the middle of the street heading for the boardwalk.

"Hey, wait a minute," yelled Peter, running along behind him. "You want me to—"

"Yeah, come on."

"How come?"

"How come what?"

"How come you got the day off? I mean, what about Muppy?"

"What about her?"

Peter ran around in front of Thad, turning to face him, walking backwards. "Don't you have to watch her and stuff?"

"Let Bridget do it today. Yeah, today I have a day off."

Thad followed Peter, listening to the sound of his tennis shoes against the street. He walked in a wraparound kind of shock, knowing that after a while he would hurt for what he had done to Muppy. But not yet. Now there was only a well-defined sharpness around him. And for the first time that summer, Thad felt as though he were seeing things without the filter of himself.

"Come on," said Peter, as they crossed the last street before the beach, "I'll race you to the boardwalk."

They stood for a moment at the top of the ramp, feeling the wind from the ocean against their faces. Then without saying anything, they turned and started to jog toward the southern end of the boardwalk. They overtook old ladies carrying shopping bags and children eating ice cream cones; they ducked in and out of families trundling across the boardwalk at every street carrying beach balls and blankets; they dodged the boardwalk train as it went by. They stared at the faces of the people lined on benches and watched old men in green high-back rockers on hotel porches and girls wearing T-shirts that said "Touch me" and "Hands off."

Thad's feet seemed to skim along, carrying him

effortlessly over the worn gray boards underfoot; past dumpsters swarming with flies. He saw cottages: sun-bleached yellow and shingled brown. He passed the Alaska stand and the Candy Corner and the Bingo Hall; passed T-shirts hung on racks and a girl making leather headbands and a sand sculptor shaping a lion. And it was as though the two boys melded into one, their feet hitting the boards in unison: thud and squeak and thud. As they got closer to the southern end of town, the cottages disappeared, seemed to crouch back away from the boardwalk, with stores and food stands pushing out in front. All around them surged the smell of French fries and pizza. They heard the tinny sound of music and the pop-pop-pop from a shooting gallery.

"Wow," said Peter, stopping short. "It's hot."

"And I'm starving," said Thad.

They ate pizzas, leaning on a counter speckled with crumbs, and drank giant root beers out of paper cups. They ate ice cream and soft pretzels and watched the mechanical man stirring a vat of saltwater taffy in a store window.

Inside the arcade the music engulfed them in a kind of rinky-dink cocoon. Peter jumped in front of a mirror, waving his arms and stretching his neck. Thad stood in back of him and they leered at themselves growing tall and spindly legged. Without speaking they moved sideways to the next mirror and saw themselves grow short and squat.

"The bumper cars," they said at once. And they were off, each stepping into his own car, careening around the floor, slamming one another backwards and forwards and sideways. They bounced off the tires that lined the walls and the air was filled with the smell of oil and rubber.

They ran outside to the Matterhorn, Peter climbing into the car first, Thad squeezing in beside him. They saw the faces on the ground blur as the car took off, circling, pulsing up and down, swinging them out so that they were riding sideways. The ride came to an end and for a minute the world seemed to swirl around them.

They rode the Wild Mouse, holding their breath as the car inched slowly upwards, and their stomachs as they dropped crazily down the other side. The ground swayed beneath them and they walked slowly past the kiddie rides and back out onto the boardwalk, testing their legs like sailors long at sea.

"I'm hungry again," said Thad, reaching into his pocket. "I have just about enough for an ice cream."

"Yeah, me too, but first I got to sit down," said Peter staggering towards a bench.

The sun, high in the sky, beat down upon them and they stretched their legs out in front. There was an all-rightness about the day, and Thad held it carefully.

Suddenly the words that Thad had been holding on to all summer long broke loose and seemed to go racing on without him. And just as suddenly Thad wanted to let them go. Without turning, he said, "Hey Peter, you know what . . . I mean about my father . . . He's in Allenwood—in prison. He—"

"Yeah," said Peter. "My mom told me about that. Pretty rough, huh?"

For a few minutes neither Thad nor Peter spoke. They just sat together watching the people on the boardwalk go up and down, up and down.

"Look," said Peter, jolting forward, "look over there."

Thad peered through the web of people, across the boardwalk. He saw a painted skeleton lurching against the wall, and two crooked tombstones flanking the double door with a turnstile in front. He saw the letters, bold and white against the black front: HOUSE OF TERROR—ENTER AT YOUR OWN RISK. A large rubber spider swung in the breeze.

"Yeah, so what?"

"Look at the sign, the little sign, in the skeleton's hand."

Thad looked again. Saw the words "Help Wanted" lettered in red.

"Yeah?" he said to the empty bench beside him. Peter was through the crowd, leaning close to the skeleton, jangling his arms and legs at the painted spook.

"It says 'Apply next-door. Ask for Carl,'" he

62

said, flopping back on the bench. "Man, that's what I call a job. Wanted, a ghoul—"

"Only disembodied spirits need apply," said Thad.

"Experienced house haunters only."

"Needed, a ghost with—"

"Go on, I dare you," said Peter jumping up and sitting on the back of the bench.

"Who me?"

"Yeah, you. You wanted a job, you said."

"Yeah, but, I got Muppy and—"

"It's not open in the day, only at night. You could. . . . You might. . . . Go ahead."

Thad stared at the skeleton and the crazily spinning spider. He looked next-door at the ice cream stand. It was hardly more than a large window framed all around with posters of mounded sundaes that swirled into enormous peaks. Paper napkins and cardboard trays from French fries had blown up against the base of the stand and hung there, flattened, flickering around the edges. A man in a gauze shirt leaned on the counter, carelessly flicking at flies with a rag.

"You think that's Carl?" he asked.

"Got to be," said Peter, nudging him with the toe of his shoe. "Go on, what're you waiting for? I tell you it's made to order."

"Well," said Thad, inching forward on the bench. "I don't know. . . ."

"I'll bet you," said Peter. "You get the job, I'll pay for the ice cream. You don't get the job, you pay for the ice cream. OK? Just march on up and all you say is 'Pardon me, sir, but I saw your sign . . .' "

Thad tried the words inside his head, testing them to see how they would sound. Shoving his hands down into his pockets, he walked up to the stand, hearing Peter snorting on the bench behind him.

The man behind the counter was making a sundae, forcing ice cream out of the chrome machine against the wall and spooning chocolate sauce over the top. The ice cream in the yellow plastic cup looked mushy and kind of slipped down, not sharp and swirled like the sundae in the picture. A fly buzzed down onto a smudge of chocolate on the counter.

He found himself staring at the man, almost as though he were looking at a picture on the wall. He studied the man's build, slight and hollow, his un-sunburned skin and the lank blond hair that fell over one eye. The shirt was transparent and slightly gray, showing a hairless chest.

"You want something, kid?"

Thad started and looked around, then realized the man was talking to him. "Uh, yes . . . er, yeah, a job. I want a job. The sign next-door said 'See Carl.' Are you?—"

64

"Yeah, I'm Carl. Wife runs this place. I'm next door. I help her out some during the day. How old are you kid?"

"Sixteen. Yeah, sixteen." Thad stood up as tall as he could and wondered what to do with his hands.

Carl looked at him, slitting his eyes. "Worked before?"

"Oh sure," said Thad. "Looking for something else though. Saw the sign and. . . . Is the job filled? I mean. . . ."

Carl turned to wait on a woman with a child in a stroller, stood talking to her for a while, lighting a cigarette and blowing smoke rings down at the child. Thad twisted one leg around the other. He didn't know whether to stay, and wasn't sure how to leave.

Carl ground his cigarette out and wiped his nose on the back of his hand. "Here for the rest of the summer? Don't want you quitting on me."

"Yes sir, yeah, till after Labor Day."

"Two-fifty an hour. Five to eleven, six days a week. Can you start tonight?"

"Tonight?" Thad heard his voice rise and crack, tried to flatten it down. Excitement took hold of him. A job. Just like that. A job. "Yeah, sure. That's swell, but what, I mean what kind of job? What do I do? I mean—"

Carl shrugged and pointed next-door. "It's a spook house. You spook. You know, scare the devil

65

out of people. Yell, moan, whatever. Not afraid of the dark, are you?" And his lip curled over yellow, uneven teeth.

"Yes sir, I mean no, that's great. OK I'll—"

"Not so fast there. Need your name." And Carl pulled an envelope out of his pants pocket.

Thad felt as though the tide were going out on him, pulling against him. "Thad-St.-Clair." He slid over the words, pushing them across the counter in a jumbled rush.

"How's that again? Sinclair, you say? OK Sinclair, what's your first name?"

"Brook," said Thad, looking over his shoulder at Peter making faces behind him. "Brook," he said again, the word sounding like a slap, and Thad wondered if his voice was too loud, tried to tone it down. "That's right, Brook Sinclair." He watched Carl write it in stubby letters on the envelope. Brook Sinclair.

"OK Sinclair, see you at five, and come around the back way." And he turned away from Thad, wiping the front of the ice cream machine with the rag.

"You got it," said Peter, slapping him on the back. "I told you. What kind of ice cream do you want?"

"No, not now. I'll take it later. Got to get home. Don't know what my mom'll say. . . ." And he pushed Peter along, away from the man named

Carl, who just might call him Brook Sinclair out loud.

They started back down the boardwalk. Away from the stores and the squawk of music, past the cottages and the hotels where the men sat in rocking chairs and stared at the ocean.

A job. A real job. All mine. Brook Sinclair. Sinclair. A job. The thoughts raced and pulled at Thad until gradually he felt a kind of unnumbing, felt the first edge of the aftershock of pain.

"We missed you at breakfast, Thad," his mother said when she came in from work. "You should have come."

Thad looked at her carefully, trying to decide whether she knew why he hadn't come, then decided that she didn't, that for some reason Bridget hadn't told. He knew also that it must have been Bridget who took care of Muppy today.

"Yeah, but Mom, guess what? I got a job, a real one. Down on the boardwalk at the spook house. I'm a spook, I—"

"A job, but Thad. . . ." His mother paused, looking at him. "Well, tell me about it."

"What do you mean he has a job?" asked Bridget coming in dressed for work. "He *has* a job—taking care of Muppy. I mean, I can't, and besides—"

"What time, Thad? You know I can't leave Muppy all day and I have to be at work. And Bridget's schedule changes. Anyway she has a job."

"But Mom, it's not till five o'clock. Five till eleven and it's two-fifty an hour and—"

"It's not fair," said Bridget, heading for the steps. "He's supposed to . . . and anyway, who'd hire him?"

Ellen St. Clair looked from one to the other. "It's all right, Bridget. We'll work it out. Maybe Thad needs this job. As long as he's with Muppy during the day, as long as she leaves the beach when he does. But Thad, a spook house?"

"Well, he's just the spook for it," said Bridget going down the stairs. "Just the spook."

"Go ahead and try it, Thad. You'll need a work permit, I guess. Oh, and did you ask about getting a couple of days off in the end of August, when we go to see your father. You know I want you all to go with me this time."

Thad went to the refrigerator and took out a coke, turning to take the glass his mother held out, his eyes skimming the top of her head.

For the first time he realized that he was taller than everybody in his family, except maybe his father, who wasn't there, who didn't count. And it suddenly seemed to Thad that there wasn't enough of him to fill his body. Somehow there wasn't enough of him to go around.

CHAPTER 7

Thad looked down at the stew in front of him: the gravy running dark and brown across the plate, lumps of carrots and potatoes staring back at him like white and yellow eyes, the steam clouding upwards. He speared a piece of meat and held it out in front of him, then dropped the fork and saw gravy splatter across the white tabletop. He pushed the plate away.

His stomach grabbed and knotted.

"I'm not hungry. It's too early, and besides, stew at four o'clock?"

His mother looked out from behind her newspaper. "It's four-fifteen, and besides, you've got to eat *something*—not getting off work until eleven. You'll be starving."

"Yeah, but, I'll get something on the board-walk after a while."

He handed a chunk of meat to Barney, then another and another. And seeing that his mother was engrossed in the paper, he held the plate down and let the dog lick it clean.

"You really ought to eat, Thad. Going to be working all night you've got to keep your strength up." Ellen St. Clair shook the newspaper and folded it outwards.

"Yeah, sure Mom," said Thad running water on the plate and putting it in the dishwasher. Why do mothers always think you have to eat something? he wondered as he wiped his hands on the seat of his jeans. They stuff you one minute and tell you not to eat the whole week's worth of groceries the next.

His mother came into the kitchen. "There now, I knew you'd feel better if you ate."

Thad looked down at Barney who was care-fully licking his chops. "You're right, Mom. I got to go now. Going to be late."

"What's his name? The man you're working for?"

"I don't know—Carl something." Thad rolled the words back in his throat, making them sound low and blurred. What difference does a name make, he thought.

"And Thad," his mother went on, "I've been thinking about that two-fifty. It's not minimum

70

wage, you know. You'd better talk to him about that, and getting a work permit too. It's easier to get everything straightened out right in the beginning."

Thad turned away quickly, heading for the stairs. "Two-fifty is great. It's, you know, it's. . . ." And for a moment he saw the job and the money slipping out from under him. "Two-fifty times six hours a day is . . . that's fifteen dollars a day—fifteen dollars." And his voice cracked.

"Yes, I know. But you're entitled to more. The law says the employer has to pay the minimum wage. It's for your own protection. Better to have it on the up and up."

Thad started down the steps, calling back over his shoulder, "That's right. St. Clairs never do anything that isn't on the up and up."

And he stood for a minute, halfway down the steps, listening to the silence of the house, not sure whether he had said the words out loud.

As he passed the empty field at the corner, Thad saw a group of boys. "Hey Thad," someone yelled, "we're getting up a game. Want to play?"

Putting his head up, he shoved his hands into his pockets and called over his shoulder, "Can't right now. Got to go to work. The boss'll kill me if I'm late." And he started to run towards the board-walk. Somehow, just the saying of the words, tossing them out like the football the boys had, made the job all right again.

He walked along the boardwalk purposefully, passing the late-afternoon strollers and families straggling home from the beach. He thought of Carl writing his name on the back of an envelope; then the pictures inside his head clicked and changed and he saw Carl, his draggled shirt replaced by a coat and tie, sitting behind a huge desk in a paneled office. "Well, Mr. Sinclair, what do you think about . . . would like your opinion on . . . the meeting next week."

And as he continued on, past the Bingo Hall and the Candy Corner, the two-fifty an hour—the fifteen dollars a day—blobbed and spread like an amoeba, reaching out to include all the things that he could do. He suddenly thought of the fins he had always wanted, the leash for the surfboard, of pizzas and subs and maybe a new bike. He thought of the money he could give his mother and of taking Muppy on the racer dip. Fifteen dollars a day times six days a week for the rest of the summer. . . . Thad walked faster.

Inside the House of Terror it was hot and smelled of sweat and bubble gum and suntan lotion. The dark oozed and pressed down around him, lightened only by the eerie green exit light at the end of the tunnel and the murky grayness of the fake windows streaked with cobwebs. Thad sank down on the stool inside the cage and loosened the neck of the black cape. His own clothes felt damp and sticky underneath, and he took a deep sniff of one armpit. He peeled the rubber mask off his head, turning it inside out and feeling the holes that were nose and fangs and hideous bulging eyes. He waved the mask up and down in the darkness trying to dry it, and wiped his own face with the backs of his hands. He could feel his hair in sweaty, scraggled clumps sticking out around his head.

He felt the inside of the cage around him—the plasterboard wall in back, the floor-to-ceiling bars in front, and the metal catch that opened three of the bars into a gate. He pushed the stool back a little and leaned against the wall, glad of a little breather, of a lull in the crowd.

When Thad had gotten to the House of Terror a few minutes before five, he had seen a line of people waiting out in front. He had ducked around back where Carl had been waiting, holding the monster mask and a heavy black Dracula kind of cape. "Good, Sinclair, you made it. Come on, they're waiting." And Thad had found himself propelled through the inky maze, through twists and turns, up inclines and down slopes in the floor, past rocks by the side of the wall and bare tree limbs made of plastic. He dodged clumps of Spanish moss and walked headlong into a dangling skeleton. When they got to the cage, Carl had shown him where the latch was, then unceremoniously shoved him inside.

"OK Sinclair, go to it. Scare the devil out of them. Got another kid who works the other end. You two can switch off after a while. And don't forget to grab at them, but watch it, sometimes they fight back." And Carl had disappeared into the darkness. Thad's job had begun.

He heard the sound of voices from the front end of the tunnel—the shuffling of feet, the muffled squeals and shrieks—heard the sounds coming closer. He pulled the mask down over his head, tugging it so that the eyeholes matched with his own eyes. The smell of rubber choked him for a moment and he held his breath, then pulled the mask out from his neck and gulped for air.

"Eee-er-ooh, grrrrrrr," shouted Thad, rattling the bars of his cage. "Ow—oooh, rruuh," he growled, flailing his arms through the bars. He saw the group of girls jump back, saw them, through the murkiness, as they flattened themselves against the wall, heard them screech, then sensed them shoving past him.

"Help. Let me out of here. What is it?"

Then the next group was upon him. Someone kicked him through the cage, and Thad hopped on one foot. A child started to cry, and a man spoke gruffly: "Stop that, Nancy. Stop that right now. *You* wanted to come. It's nothing, I tell you. Be a big girl."

Sometime during the night Peter had come, whooping through the tunnel, bouncing from side

74

to side, leaning close to the cage and whispering, "Wanted a spook—a disembodied spirit." And he had disappeared down past the green exit light that made him look strangely mottled, and out the door.

Thad's throat ached from yelling, and for a while he crouched down on the floor, moaning softly. He felt a hand reach in, felt someone pull at his rubber ears. Then he leapt up, snarling.

He turned away, holding out the edges of the mask to get a little air. He felt a presence close by and when he turned back, his cage was surrounded by a group of boys. He smelled their beery breath, heard the taunt in their voices. "Hey, look you guys, a real live monster. Let's get the monster." And they lashed out at him, shaking the bars from the outside, poking at him with fists and half-filled cans of beer, stomping, howling, hissing at him.

Thad pulled back against the wall, stumbling over the stool. He heard the clink of the latch and for a minute he froze, then roared, lunging forward. "Arrroooooo. . . ."

From somewhere in the back a voice called. "Hey, keep it moving up there. Others are waiting. Move along." Thad felt a can hit him on the side of the mask, then saw the boys move on.

The crowd thinned and straggled, coming now in clumps, with spaces in between. Thad slipped out of the cape and let it drop to the floor around his feet.

And then the lights came on, bare, dim bulbs

that hung from the ceiling, making everything look raw and tawdry. Thad pushed his way through the gate and headed for the door.

Carl stood on the outside steps next to the crooked tombstones, talking to a group of men. For a few minutes Thad stood on the edge of the crowd, waiting for Carl to speak to him, to catch his eye, to tell him how well he'd done. The men talked and laughed and slapped each other on the back and then drifted off one by one. Carl ground his cigarette out and turned, nodding briefly to Thad, as if not at all sure who he was, then headed back into the empty spook house.

From then on, Thad's days foreshortened into just the nights. It was as if nothing else mattered: his time at home, taking Muppy to the beach, his life with his mother and Bridget—especially with Peter out most days crewing on the *Kitty Hawk*. It seemed as though the day began at five o'clock and ended sometime after eleven as he walked down the boardwalk eating an ice cream cone and feeling the wind dry his sweaty clothes.

He got to know the people in the stores around the spook house—the pizza maker and the ice cream man and the artist who did portraits in charcoal. During his break he ran next door, and Carl's wife, Doris, gave him a Coke and asked him how it was going. And sometimes he walked home with Tim, the boy who worked the front end of the tunnel, stopping along the way to play the pinball machines.

But mostly the pattern stayed the same: the snarling and roaring and the clanging of bars, the crowds and the heat and the suffocating dark, and Carl lurking on the edges, watery-eyed and pale, with never much to say.

Thad found, as he sat in the cage on the fifth night at work, that he was inventing games, trying to think of ways to make the time go faster. It was raining outside and the crowd was sparse.

It all started with the older woman. Thad saw her, tall and imposing, through the shadows. He smelled her perfume and heard her talking to the children with her. Something about the woman pulled and tugged at him: something about the precision of her words, clipped and cold, and the way she seemed to draw in upon herself and hurry the children along. Her scent lingered after her, and suddenly, to Thad, it was as though his grandmother had stood on the outside of the cage peering in at him.

And then a whole parade of people marched in front of Thad. Cardboard, make-believe people, superimposed on the regular crowd. Thad found himself growling at his supposed grandmother, trying to shatter the iciness that had turned her against his father. He shook the bars at the auditors of the Savings and Loan and rasped at his father's boss. He clawed at the judge, reaching his arm through the bars.

It was as though he were caught in a riptide,

fighting against all the hurt and anger that held him there.

Then he saw his father's face, looming in front of him, watery-eyed and pale from months in prison, saw him through the bars of his own cage.

"Arrreugh, grrrrr," shouted Thad, throwing his shoulder against the cage.

The beam from a flashlight caught him in the face. "OK kid, you're doing great, a terrific job," said Carl. "But don't waste it on me. Just wanted to tell you we're closing early tonight. It's pouring outside. Only thing we'll get tonight is ducks. Get on home now."

CHAPTER 8

"Come on Thad, let's go. Let's *do* something. We've been here for hours just looking at those dumb old fins." Muppy twisted herself around in the curtain that hung in front of the dressing room, encasing herself like a mummy, with only her head and legs showing. "Come *on,* Thad." She pushed herself around, trying to unwind to the beat and throb of the music from the stereo behind the counter.

Untangling herself, she wandered over to the wet suits hanging along one wall, shaking their arms and nodding to their headless shapes. She ran her fingers across the surfboards, then stopped before a mirror and held a bikini up to herself, wiggling her hips backwards and forwards.

Muppy sat cross-legged on the floor and stared

up at Thad. "Let's go, for Pete's sake. You said one minute and then we'd go to the beach and it's been forever. First you hold up the blue fins and then the black fins; then you hold them up to your feet, then you look at the price again, then you look like you're adding stuff in your head, and I bet you don't have any money anyway so—"

"I will—tonight, it's payday. I just wanted to pick them out so tomorrow all I have to do is come in and pay and—"

"Shall I put them aside for you?" asked the teen-aged girl coming out from behind the counter. "They go so fast, and I'd be happy to save a pair. . . ." Muppy listened to the girl's breathless voice, heard it nudging at Thad.

Thad dropped the blue fins. Then he dropped the black ones. He pushed the hair out of his eyes and tried to wipe away a pimple that seemed to throb and swell on the end of his chin. He bent to retrieve the fins, bumping into a display of Sea and Ski and sending plastic bottles and tubes skimming across the floor.

"Yikes," said Thad crawling around the floor, scrabbling after the Sea and Ski. "Yeah, great. I mean I get paid tonight. Tomorrow I'll . . . Muppy don't just stand there—help!"

Muppy dropped to her hands and knees and sidled up to Thad. She made her breath come in little spurts as she said, "Shall I put them aside for

80

you? I'd just *love* to." Then she scooted off as Thad made a lunge for her. "Go on, get lost. Wait for me outside. I just have to—"

Muppy pulled at the door, setting off a jangle of bells. "I'll be on the boardwalk, but hurry up; it might rain. Tru-weather said—"

"Don't worry about that stuff," the girl's voice wisped. "I'll do something with it later. Just tell me what fins and your name. I can only hold them two days." She nibbled the end of a pencil.

"The blue, I guess. Yeah, the blue," said Thad putting the large rubber fins on the counter. "I get my paycheck tonight so I can get them first thing in the morning. I'll be here when you open. I'll . . . guess you'll be closed tonight . . . when I get off work I mean. Otherwise I'd come then."

"Just give me your name, OK?" said the girl, as she started to sort a box of hangers behind the counter. "This your first job or something?"

"Thad St. Clair. I, uh, no . . . had all kinds of jobs. We're here every summer." Thad heard his voice spinning ahead of him, dipping and cracking, felt his eyes riveted on the front of the girl's T-shirt. "I mean . . . had my eyes on these fins for ages. You might know my sister Bridget, works at the Crab House. You want anything else, I mean address, phone number, you know. . . ."

"Nope, that's it. Two days, though. That's all I can hold them. See you." She turned back to the jumbled mess of hangers, her body moving slightly to the music.

"You're early, kid," said Carl, looking up from his place on the back steps, his yellow eyes squinting against the late afternoon sun.

"Yeah, I guess," said Thad, leaning against the side of a dumpster. "Clock was wrong or something."

"Can't stay away, huh? No overtime on this job, kid." Thad felt his face turning hot and red. He turned his head away, watching a bee hovering over a half-eaten ice cream cone in the alley. For a minute he felt that Carl could see inside his head, see the strange fascination that seemed to draw him here earlier and earlier, and make him hang around after the lights went on and the House of Terror turned shabby and small.

"Well Sinclair, might as well make yourself useful." Carl's voice twanged like rubber bands. "Go around front and get us a piece of pizza. Here, catch." He tossed a wad of money to Thad.

Thad stood in line at the pizza place. "Get us a piece of pizza," Carl had said. And "us" meant "both." But Thad wasn't sure. Maybe it was just an expression. Maybe what he really meant was get *me* a piece of pizza. Thad unfolded the money and looked at the five dollar bill. Plenty of money for two, but still. Thad shifted from one foot to the next as the line moved up. If he meant one and Thad bought two or if he meant two and, . . . "I could always say I wasn't hungry," thought Thad, breathing in cheese and sauce and pepperoni and mushrooms. He heard his stomach growl. "Two pieces with the works," he said to the man behind the counter. But at the last minute he paid for Carl's pizza out of the five and dug in his pocket for his own money to pay for his.

Carl slid over on the steps to make room for Thad, and for a minute they ate in silence, the strings of cheese stretching like rubber and swaying slightly in the breeze. Over the spice of the pizza, Thad smelled Carl's aftershave, chokingly sweet. He saw the phony diamond ring flashing on his finger. Carl poked him with his elbow, at the same time wiping his mouth on the back of his hand. "Pretty good, huh kid. You like that?"

"Yeah, great, terrific. Thanks a lot," said Thad, handing Carl the change and wondering, all of a sudden, why he was thanking him for the pizza he had paid for himself.

"Oh, hey kid, speaking of money, I got your paycheck here." Carl dragged a wilted envelope out of his pocket and handed it to Thad.

"Boy, that's great. I can use it." And Thad had to bite his tongue to keep from telling Carl about the fins he had on hold, and about the money he wanted to give his mother, and how he was going to take Muppy on the Wild Mouse and. . . .

83

"Need it, my ass," said Carl standing up and running a comb through his slicked back hair. "You kids are all alike. I can tell by looking at you you don't need nothing. Got the world by the tail, eh Sinclair? Move it now; time for work. What's your old man do, anyways?"

Thad turned away and shoved the envelope down in his pocket. As he turned back, Carl was standing by the open back door. "OK Sinclair, get a move on it. Time for work."

Then Thad was swallowed up by the darkness of the haunted house, pushing his way into the cage and putting on the cape and mask. The crowds came through the maze, shoving and screaming, flapping arms at Thad's rubber face as he snarled and growled back at them.

Hot, dark, and sticky, the night edged on. Every once in a while Thad patted the pay envelope inside his pocket. All around him the voices formed a skein of sound, tangling and winding over him, until from the direction of the entrance he became aware of one voice louder than the rest. It was as though someone had hold of a string, pulling and tugging it, unraveling everything around him.

"Thad, Thad St. Clair." Thad recognized Muppy's voice, heard every syllable as though it were a shot. "Thad, hey, Thad-e-us St. Clair, where are you? I know you're in here. Come on, scare us."

The voice got closer, swelling, bouncing off the walls and filling the tunnel around him.

84

"Thad-e-us St. Clair Junior, Thad, hey, Thad."

And running as if in counterpoint came the thin, high voice of Muppy's friend Jenny. "Hey Thad, where are you? Come on, spook."

"Thad the spook. Hey, we came all the way up here to see you. We asked the guy out front and he said. . . ."

Thad rattled the bars of his cage, trying to drown out the girls' voices. What guy outside, he thought, wondering where Carl was, whether he had heard. Was it Carl the girls had asked? Carl was taking tickets while the regular man was on a break. Or was Carl somewhere in the tunnel hearing the name Thadeus St. Clair being flung around. Maybe he wouldn't know. No reason for him to think that Thad St. Clair and Brook Sinclair were the same. Just some crazy kids carrying on, looking for some-one. And suddenly Thad remembered Carl's slitted yellow eyes and how he asked, "What's your old man do, anyways?"

"Augrrrrgh," bellowed Thad, shaking the bars as he saw a shadowed Muppy and Jenny round the corner. He reached out and grabbed his sister's arm and pulled her close to the cage, hissing out at her, "Hey Muppy, shut up. What're you trying to do? You're going to blow my cover. Nobody's supposed to know who I am. I'm the spook and spooks don't have names."

"But Thad, we came to see you. We wanted to—"

85

"Well here I am. Pretend you don't know me. It works better. Tell you what, you go on, you and Jenny and I'll take you on the Wild Mouse tomorrow."

"Will you take me crabbing?" asked Muppy, pulling away from Thad. "Will you?"

From behind them came the shuffle of feet and the jumble of voices.

"Hey beat it, you two. People're coming. I got to work."

Thad saw Muppy's eyes staring at him through the dark. "Go on Muppy. The Wild Mouse, yeah, OK, and crabbing too."

"Grrrr—awoughhhh," shrieked Thad as Muppy and Jenny turned and ran towards the door.

Thad didn't wait for the lights to go on after work. Dropping the cape and mask on the floor of the cage, he ran towards the door. Carl was nowhere in sight, and Thad called good-night to Doris as he headed down the boardwalk.

Thad went several blocks before he stopped, flopping down on an empty bench under a street light. He pulled the envelope out of his pocket and held it up in front of him, letting the edges flap in the breeze, savoring the very existence of it. He wiggled his toes inside his shoes and thought of how tomorrow he would have his fins, good ones with the elongated piece on the outside of each foot—the kind the real body surfers wore. He looked out at the dark ocean and tensed the muscles in his legs, and for a moment he could feel himself sweeping through the water.

The glue on the envelope gave way easily, and Thad slipped the check out, anchoring it with his fingers against the wind. His salary: two-fifty an hour times six hours a day times six days a week.

Thad froze.

In the distance he heard the pounding of the surf and behind him he heard the footsteps of the late night strollers. But the rest of his body was numb: deadened, petrified, turned to stone or wood or molded plastic. His hand-lumps held the check and the words throbbed up at him.

Pay to the order of BROOK SINCLAIR.

It was as though a hundred waves came down on him, pounding and smashing and driving into him. And still Thad sat unmoving and stared at the check. After a while he shoved it back into his pocket and stood up, the muscles inside his body screaming as though they had not been used for a long, long time. And he started home, the thoughts reeling inside of him.

Pay to the order of . . . but I'm not Brook Sinclair. There isn't any Brook Sinclair. But I am . . . I did . . . I worked for it . . . just sign my name . . . that name. Who's to know . . . what difference. St. Clair, Sinclair . . . the same, the. . . .

Something clawed inside of him and his body iced with sweat. To sign his name, to sign not-his-name on something. There was a word, "forgery," but was it forgery for his own money. His two-fifty an hour: not his but Brook Sinclair's—but there was no Brook Sinclair. Would he go to jail? To prison? Be locked up? And the thing inside of Thad's stomach dug deeper and tore at him. Did it run in families? Was he . . . like his father?

Bridget and his mother were in the living room watching a late movie.

"Hi Thad, did you get your check?" his mother called.

"Yeah, sure." And Thad headed for the refrigerator trying to drown his mother's voice with the rattle and clink of catsup bottles and pickle jars.

"Let me see it—your first paycheck."

Thad listened to the gentle hum of the refrigerator and stared at a curl of jelly on the edge of a jar. "Aw Mom, it's no big deal, just a check."

"Close the refrigerator. But Thad, it's all right, isn't it? I mean that man didn't cheat you, did he? Did you get it straight about the minimum wage? Maybe I should talk to him."

Bridget reached over Thad's shoulder and took an apple. "Come on, Mom. Leave him alone. Stop babying him, for heaven's sake. Thad can take care of himself." Heading for the steps, she called "Somebody wake me up *early*. T.J. and I are going waterskiing in the morning."

CHAPTER 9

The knocker on the front door sounded like an angry woodpecker, and Thad pulled a pillow down over his head. But still the sound persisted: tap, tap, tap, tap, tap—pushing through the web of sleep and folded pillow. Why doesn't Muppy get that door, thought Thad, burrowing deeper into the bed before he remembered that Muppy had spent the night at Jenny's.

Tap, tap, tap came the sound again. "Leave it and go away," yelled Thad, pulling the spread from the top bunk down and wrapping it around his head.

He knew it was the newsgirl from down the street, tiny and persistent. No matter how careful his mother was to pay her in advance, no matter how often they told her to leave the paper under the mat, she insisted on beating her tatoo every morning.

Tap, tap, tap. . . .

He heard Bridget go to the door and settled down for another sleep. The room was cool and shadowed. Thad stretched out, pushing his feet against the bottom of the bed and shoving the extra spread onto the floor. From out on the bay came the roar of a powerboat. Thad flopped over onto his stomach and felt the threads of sleep slip away from him. He heard the sound of Bridget's shower, then heard his sister going up the stairs. From overhead came footsteps and the slam of the refrigerator door.

Something nagged at Thad, some idea that he should be up and doing something, going someplace, getting. . . . Then he remembered the fins and how he had told the girl he would pick them up this morning, and how his check said Brook Sinclair, and how he knew he was never going to be able to cash it.

Thad folded his arms over his eyes, but still the fins nudged their way in, darting from one side of his eyelids to the other, bouncing and spiraling like dust motes in sunshine.

The screen door slammed and he heard the crowding and overlapping of voices. "Come on Bridget . . . hurry up . . . have to meet the others . . . water skis and. . . ."

Thad heard the voices changing, shifting gears as it were, arguing. "Come on, we'll wait. We've had it planned. . . ."

The door slammed again, and Thad heard the

revving of a car engine and the spit of gravel.

It was as if the silence of the house crept in around him, pushing under the door and past the window frame, intruding on him through the floor and ceiling and walls. It was a silence so tangible he could almost touch it, a silence that prodded him awake instead of lulling him to sleep.

Thad rolled out of bed and pulled on a pair of jeans. As he opened his door, the silence was stronger and more palpable, pushing against him as he climbed the steps. It was a stillness, but not an emptiness: a being, a presence that had consumed all trace of sound. Waiting. Waiting.

Bridget sat crumpled on the couch, doubled over, rocking gently back and forth. Thad was aware of his sister, saw her there, but saw her as if from a distance. He was suddenly more conscious of the things around him: the percolator that spewed coffee fumes out into the room; the piece of toast poking starkly out of the toaster; Bridget's red and white striped beach towel heaped on the table. And Thad had to pull his attention back to Bridget, force himself to concentrate on the gently swaying body on the yellow vinyl couch, and to hear the low moans that were beginning to fill the room.

He suddenly felt as though he were spying, in-truding, staring at a rawness that up until then had been no part of his sister as he had known her.

Thad backed down the stairs, banging against

91

the wall at the bottom and singing "Camelot" in a haphazard voice and taking the steps two at a time.

But it hadn't made any difference. Bridget was still crouched in the same position, folded over the newspaper with her arms clutched across her stomach. And she was crying.

Thad had never seen Bridget cry. He stood rooted, playing a kind of trivia game with himself, pushing back into their childhood. He saw Bridget angry, red-faced and furious; he saw Bridget hurt, his mind clicking through a series of skinned knees and barked elbows; he saw her sullen, impatient, frustrated. But in that whole long stretch of emotions, he had never seen his sister cry, had in fact always seen her swathed in a thin coat of detachment.

And now Bridget sat on the yellow couch and cried, and Thad stood first on one foot and then the other and wondered what to do.

"Hey . . . uh . . . I mean . . . hey Bridge, is anything wrong?" Suddenly Thad felt that he had too many arms and legs and nothing to do with any of them. "Hey, what the—"

"It's here, the whole thing, all over again. All over the papers, and that picture." Bridget's voice rose to a wail reaching to all the corners of the room and out through the open windows. She stood up, her face streaked with tears, and shoved the newspaper at Thad. "And, and they're suing him—Dad—

because of the money they had to pay the Savings and Loan and, and—"

"Who's suing . . . what . . . I don't. . . ." But Thad found that for a moment his reactions were muted by his surprise at Bridget. He dropped the paper onto the table, smoothing and flattening it. He watched the print make black smudges on the white of the tabletop and seemed to see Bridget walking unscathed through months between his father's arraignment and eventual sentencing.

His hands worked on the paper as if they were not a part of him, straightening the edges and reassembling the pages until there was nothing left to do. In the background Bridget's tears subsided and spent themselves.

The story was on the front page of the paper: one of the papers brought down by truck in the dark of the early morning for vacationers to have with their morning coffee. A front-page story, three-column head, a funny, blurred picture of the St. Clair family taken years before, a mother and father herding a younger Bridget, Thad, and Muppy down the steps away from a grandfather's funeral. And as though time had stopped, they marched again across the front of the newspaper.

Thad tried to skim the article, but found his eyes snagged by certain words and phrases: "The Mid-Atlantic Surety Company today filed suit in Circuit Court against Thadeus Brook St. Clair. . . .

alleged embezzlement of funds amounting to . . . Emblem Federal Savings and Loan . . . prominent family . . . grandson of the late Governor Martin J. St. Clair . . . married to . . . three children . . . member of the fashionable Blue Valley Country Club . . . presenting serving time . . . Allenwood, Pa. . . .

Then wildly, crazily, the words and phrases that rose up starkly in black and white seemed to take on new dimensions, to add color and substance, to summon up other times and places. Thad's head ached with yards of film that seemed to be running through his mind: wound and broken and spliced and tangled. He remembered his mother saying how the bonding company would sue for the money they had paid on his father's behalf; then something switched and he saw his family leaving his grandfather's funeral, the day the picture was taken; and then he was back in time to a smaller Thad being taken by the hand to see his dead great grandfather, the governor, and wondering what a governor was. He saw his grandmother and remembered Sunday brunches at the Blue Valley Country Club after his father's golf game. And one scene was more sharply focused than the rest: his mother and father on either end of an argument, with his mother saying, "We don't need the Club . . . can't afford . . ." and his father answering, "The St. Clairs have always been charter members. . . ." "No reason now. . . ." "Always a good reason. . . ."

Thad folded the paper over, then over again, trying to make it look unread, unused. He was aware of Bridget brushing her hair, and watched her divide it into sections and braid it, watched her fold her self-assurance into the long blond plaits.

"That's the pits, isn't it?" said Bridget, looking up and shrugging, but already, it seemed to Thad, her voice was edged with remoteness. It was as if by bundling the newspapers off to him she had waived her part in the situation. It was almost as if he could see her piecing the shield back around herself.

"Yeah," said Thad, "it's rotten dragging it all back up. And Mom, I guess she saw it. You know how she reads the paper at work."

Downstairs the door slammed and they could hear people crowding into the hall. "Hey Bridget, you up there? We're all going. . . ."

Bridget dove across the room and grabbed the paper, shoving it under a sofa cushion.

Suddenly the room was filled with people, swirling, milling, jostling. "Going clamming over by Watch Island," a tall blond boy said. And other voices added, "Come on with us Bridget . . . thought you were going water skiing this morning . . . took a chance and stopped by."

Thad saw Bridget in the center of the group, laughing, tossing her head, her voice arching over the rest: "Really glad you came. Feel as though I might make it now. Boy, was I hung over, and when

T.J. came, no way. Had to send him on. Come on, let's go."

As quickly as they had come, they were gone, and Thad was alone in the room. For a few minutes he wasn't sure of anything, until out from under the edge of the yellow vinyl sofa cushion he saw the corner of the newspaper. There was a feeling that came over him at times, like a terrible recurring dream, and it settled down on him now, uneasy and vague. It was a feeling that Bridget was inching herself away from them, and that one day she would remove herself completely from the rest of them. And like a recurring dream, he was never really free of it, as if it waited for him just below the surface. It left a kind of loneliness around him.

Thad pulled the newspaper out from under the cushion and shredded it into hundreds of tiny pieces. He shoved them down into the trash can under coffee grounds and Pepsi cans. Then he took cleanser on a rag and scrubbed at the newspaper print smudges on the tabletop, as if the stains could somehow reassemble themselves into a news story superimposed there on the table for Muppy to see. It's good we're going crabbing, thought Thad. Just to make sure Muppy doesn't see it. S'bad enough for the rest of us, but . . . To be on the safe side, Thad picked up the trash can and started to take it out to the garbage.

Muppy shot into the room. She dropped her duffel bag onto the table and crawled over the back of the couch reaching down behind it. "Don't talk to me; don't say a word." The words sounded jumble-mouthed as she resurfaced and settled down in the corner of the couch, opening the book of *Grimm's*.

"I forgot last night but Jenny's mother said it would be OK if I read my story right now and then read another one tonight and it wouldn't break the pattern and all. And besides it's all your fault Thad, 'cause if I hadn't been in such a hurry to get to the House of Terror then I wouldn't have forgotten the book when I packed my stuff and I didn't remember it until this morning when I was halfway through my French toast. But Jenny's mother said I might as well finish and then come home and read it, so stop talking to me and let me finish."

Thad shook his head and stared at Muppy for a few minutes, watching her turn the pages and push at the nosepiece of her glasses with her index finger. He fixed himself a bowl of cereal and sat down to eat.

Muppy closed the book with a sigh. *"Briar Rose,"* she said. "But tonight is *Juniper Tree* and that's really long so I guess I better take it with me."

She circled the room slowly, pushing books and magazines aside and pulling the curtains away from the windowsills.

"What're you doing?" asked Thad, putting the milk away. Muppy disappeared into the bathroom

97

and then came out again. "Doing? I'm not doing anything," she said, going out onto the porch.

"You going to take that book crabbing?" asked Thad, getting out the bread to make peanut butter and jelly sandwiches.

"Crabbing?" screeched Muppy. "I don't want to go crabbing today. I want to go—"

"For Pete's sake, all you've talked about is going crabbing. 'Come on Thad, let's go crabbing. Please Thad.' And last night you said . . . made me promise. . . . Come on, Muppy. We're going crabbing."

"Well, if I said then I can unsaid. I really truly want to go to the beach today," said Muppy doing a backward roll across the living room and looking under the couch as she did it. "It's too hot to go crabbing. It's roasting and steaming and—"

"OK, OK. Get your suit on," said Thad looking warily at the trash can. "We'll go to the beach."

"Oh neat," said Muppy heading down towards her bedroom to change. "And besides Thad, did you forget? This is the day you have to pick up your fins."

CHAPTER 10

Thad jumped off the boardwalk onto the sand and started across the beach.

"But *why not* Thad?" asked Muppy, following along behind him. "I thought you wanted them. I thought that's why we spent hours in the Surf Shop yesterday just looking at fins and you told that girl with the twitchy backside to put the fins aside and you'd be back today, and anyway, Peter has some. Hey, wait up."

Thad turned around suddenly, and Muppy smacked into the middle of him.

"Look, Muppy, it's like this: all that money. I mean, when I got my paycheck . . . I don't know, it kind of looked like so much, I just don't want to spend it. I'm going to put it in the bank and get interest and watch it grow. And maybe be a millionaire or something."

"Hey, Thad, over here. Where've you been?" Thad turned around slowly, trying to find the voice. He saw Pat and Bill waving and beckoning to him over by the beach stand.

"You going to work there?" asked Muppy spreading her towel and flopping down right where she stood.

"Well, I might for a while, if they want. Where's Jenny?"

"At the store with her mother. But that's OK 'cause I've got something to do. Go on."

Standing for a moment and tunneling into the sand with his left foot, Thad wondered if Pat and Bill had seen the story in the morning paper. Remembering how they usually arrived for work half-asleep, he doubted it and shrugged and started across the beach.

Business was slow. The umbrellas were already up, and because of the riptide hardly anyone came to rent surf mats. Thad knew that the ocean was rough just by the way the lifeguard kept blowing his whistle and waving swimmers away from the jetty. Somehow, even though Bill and Pat had gone to lunch, Thad couldn't settle down. He felt restless, jumping every time the whistle blew and standing up a couple of times to see what was happening.

100

Suddenly, without really thinking about it, he found he was watching Muppy. First she walked slowly around the beach, circling families on blankets and old ladies in folding chairs. She stepped over corners of towels and ducked under the row of umbrellas. At first Thad thought she was looking for someone, but at times it looked to him almost as if she was stalking a prey. He saw her approach a large blue trash can and saw her disappear from the waist up as she rummaged around inside. When she reappeared she went on slowly patrolling the beach, occasionally stopping for a minute, then moving on. After a while Thad noticed that she had settled down a few feet behind a man in a dark-green canvas sand chair. She crouched, folded in upon herself, like a cat watching a bird. The lifeguard's whistle continued to bleat, and a small plane cruised out over the water trailing a banner: The Chicken Coop—All you can eat—$4.95. The man in the green canvas chair stood up and stretched and headed for the trash can. Muppy circled quickly down by the water, arriving just a few steps behind him. Once again Thad saw the top half of her disappear into the trash.

Just then Pat and Bill were back, stepping between Muppy and Thad, talking, laughing. "Thanks Thad. How's your job going? Big crowds up there?" Pat flipped a fifty-cent piece in Thad's direction. "Here, get yourself a Coke, and thanks again."

When Thad looked again, the blue trash can stood alone and glistening in the sunlight and Muppy was nowhere in sight. He threw the coin in the air and caught it, heading for the boardwalk. Just as he got to the top of the ramp, he stopped and swung around, trying to hunch down inside his shirt, and looking out to sea as if he were Balboa discovering the Pacific. He sneaked a glance over his shoulder, then leaped over the railing and back onto the sand. The girl from the Surf Shop had been walking down the boardwalk, coming straight towards him. Thad flopped down onto the beach and sat for a minute holding his breath, half expecting the girl to follow him down onto the sand, wanting to know why he hadn't come in for the fins, demanding the money. Gradually he became aware of Muppy flattening something inside the *Grimm's*. Sheets of newspaper swirled and flapped around her, catching in the wind and taking off down the beach. Before Thad could ask her where she had been and what she was doing, she scurried after the papers, scooping them up and heading back to the trash can.

In an instant Thad felt cold and heavy. He picked up Muppy's book, flipping through until he found the picture. It was folded once and the edges were torn and ragged, but it was there: the three of them and his mother and father. And Thad knew what Muppy had been looking for as she paced the beach.

"Well nobody tells me anything," she said defensively as she sat on her rumpled towel and pulled the book away from Thad. "And this morning at Jenny's I saw that, or thought I saw it, and then there was Jenny's mother grabbing up the papers and running them out to the dumpster and not even making me and Jenny do it. And then I got home, and . . ."

Thad wanted to back away from the conversation. He wanted to yell, "Last one in's a rotten egg" and head for the water, or head back up to the boardwalk. Even the girl from the Surf Shop couldn't make him feel as awful as Muppy made him feel. She sat cross-legged with the book on her lap and the picture spread out on top of the book. Thad watched as she flicked a few grains of sand away and outlined her father's body with her finger.

"We could give him some money," Muppy said. "I've got two dollars and twenty-seven cents and. . . ."

Oh God, groaned Thad to himself. She read it too. And for once he wished Muppy wasn't quite as smart as she was.

He wanted to edge away from her, pretend he hadn't heard. Instead, he heard himself saying, "It's a lot of money, Muppy. An awful lot. If he could have paid it back, he would have. There isn't that much money. I mean for us there isn't."

"We could sell something."

"Nothing much to sell." Again Thad felt that he wanted to inch away, to distract Muppy with an ice cream cone or an Italian ice. But suddenly, from somewhere far away, beyond himself, he had the feeling that he owed her more than that. He stayed where he was and watched Muppy as she cupped her chin in her hands and stared down at the picture.

"The house—we could sell the house." Muppy slammed the book and put it aside as if she had settled everything.

"Can't. House isn't ours."

"What do you mean it isn't ours?" Muppy yelped. "We always lived in that house. Forever. And now we'll sell it and—"

"It's in trust. Grandfather left his house and another one, the one we live in, in trust, and it stays that way. Grandmother couldn't even sell it even if she wanted to—which she wouldn't. It stays like that until she dies."

Muppy took off her glasses and rubbed them on the edge of the towel, then blew on them to get the sand off. "Well, I guess . . . I mean . . . well, Grandmother looks pretty healthy so we'll have to sell something else. How about this house at the beach? How about that?"

Thad felt as though he were breaking things: just like the time when he was little and had knocked over a jar of applesauce in the store and that jar had knocked over another, and another. He felt for a moment that he was drowning Muppy in applesauce.

"We don't own the beach house. They always rented it, and the only reason we're here this year is 'cause they'd signed a lease and Bridget had her job and Mom knew she could get one here, and then they could sublet the house in town and get more money and. . . ."

A cloud covered the sun and the air was suddenly cool. Thad saw goose bumps on Muppy's arm, and saw her face look pinched and suddenly small.

"Don't worry about it, Mup. It'll all work out," he said, trying to make his voice deep and wise-sounding.

Muppy pulled on her navy-blue sweat shirt; she picked up the book and held it tight. "I think I'll go home now, Thad. Maybe we should have gone crabbing after all."

Thad watched Muppy go across the beach and up over the boardwalk, dragging her towel behind her. Then he ran into the water, hurling himself into a wave, gasping at the cold. He moved further out, poising himself just where the waves were breaking. He looked over his shoulder at the water cresting in back of him, then turned quickly, in time to catch the ride. The wave propelled him along, knifing him through the water until he felt the scrape of sand and shells on his chest and he was ground against the shore. Thad lay there, spent and empty, digging his toes and fingers into the sand to keep from being pulled out by the receding water. His elbows bit into the sand and he stared down at the currents rushing backwards. Thad felt as though he were too weak to stand up, as though he were a piece of driftwood tossed against the beach. Another wave hit him from behind, pushing his head down into the sand and stinging his eyes. Thad struggled up, staggering onto the beach and dropping down onto his towel. He hung his head between his knees and watched the water dripping from his hair and nose, making dark splotches in the sand.

Thad was used to the ocean. He could stay in it for hours, riding waves, diving them, fighting it. But today he felt drained, as if someone had clipped away a corner and all his selfishness had run out. He shook the hair out of his eyes and rested his chin on his knees. The sureness he had tried to feel while he was talking to Muppy slid away from him. He thought of his conversation with Bridget that morning and how Bridget seemed to piece herself back together without his help. He thought of his mother.

Part of him wanted to do something for all of them, to take charge, to solve all their problems. Another part of him wanted to run and hide, to crouch down low and have someone else tell him things were going to be all right.

And he wanted things to be all right.

He wanted his father not to be a crook.

He wanted his father to come home and not to come home; he wanted to be able to talk to him and never to see him again. The wanting and the not wanting made him hurt inside.

106

The clock outside the Bingo Hall said four-fifteen when Thad hurried past. He had managed to get home and showered and out of the house before his mother came in from work. He had hurried so in case Peter got in early and came over, he would be gone. When he left, Muppy had been doing back-ward walkovers on the dock with Jenny and laugh-ing as though the corners of her world had been spliced together. It was as though everything was back to normal, as if there had never been any pic-ture in the morning paper, no Bridget crumpled on the sofa and no Muppy rooting in the trash.

Only Thad seemed to be out of kilter, as if he had started with his left foot instead of his right or sung when he should not have sung.

Only Thad seemed to remember the stumpy headlines and the three-column story that laid his life out bare boned and smudged his hands with ink.

He walked down the boardwalk as though he were naked, caught in one of those treadmill dreams, trapped and terribly visible. His skin itched with being stared at, and the pounding of the surf sounded like so many voices saying, "There he is— the boy whose father . . . look . . . the picture . . . the St. Clair boy. . . ."

Thad cringed and looked around quickly, but the scene on the boardwalk went on without him: a general up and down of people, none of them carry-ing newspapers, none of them staring.

But still he walked faster, hurrying to get to

work, as if the House of Terror with its plastic cobwebs and paper-maché tombstones offered him security.

Carl sat on the unpainted back step reading the paper.

Thad stopped short, backing up against a dumpster and listening to the music from the merry-go-round that drifted down the alley. He stared at the paper, folded small, and tried to tell if it were the city paper or the local weekly. Carl's fingers looked pale against the print of the newspaper, and his nails were long and shaded with dirt. After a few minutes he looked up, his eyes hooded.

"OK S-Sinclair. Should be a busy night, the volunteer firemen are in town." Thad seemed to crouch back inside himself. Carl's words sounded wet and slavered over, and Thad wondered if he had hesitated over Sinclair, had, in fact, meant to say St. Clair.

A few minutes later Carl sent the newspaper sailing into the dumpster. "Very in-ter-esting," he said, standing up and scratching his stomach.

Thad found himself dissecting the "very interesting," picking it to pieces. What was interesting? The firemen's convention, or something that he had seen in the paper? And when Carl held the back door open saying, "Come on kid, go haunt a house," Thad ducked quickly past him and into the shadowed building.

He worked his way past the plaster rocks and dodged the hanging moss. From somewhere in the back of him, Carl shouted "OK Sinclair, get in your cell where you belong."

Thad stopped outside the cage staring in, his fingers working the latch. Carl's words exploded through the maze, tunneling and pushing after him. "In your cell . . . you belong . . . Sinclair . . . St. Clair . . . in your cell. . . ."

From the front door came the sound of a group of girls giggling and shoving one another, starting through the passageway.

Thad loosened his fingers on the metal bars, pushing himself away and on towards the door where the exit light shone green and eerie.

CHAPTER 11

It was as if the running had been building up in Thad all summer, and even before, as if his insides had been wound tight with rubber bands, his legs, his thoughts, and his remembering all bound and interconnected. Everything seemed to spring loose at once, spinning, unwinding, clacketing within him.

And Thad ran.

He cut down off the boardwalk, away from the House of Terror and the throb of the Penny Arcade, across the three-block width of the town.

He turned up Bayside Drive and headed north, his feet hitting the street one and then the other, one and then. . . . The sun beat down on him, and the air around him was warm and spongy. It was as if Thad ran in a glass tunnel, and the bay on one side of the road and the houses on the other were not a part of his running. Thoughts swarmed around him like gnats, encircling and pushing down on him. And for the first time that summer Thad could not outrun them.

Suddenly the reality of the summer was dissipated and it was February again.

It was late in the afternoon; his mother had made a fire in the fireplace, and the house smelled of burning pine and wet mittens drying on the radiator. Outside, the streets were covered with ice with just two tire tracks ribboned in black. Bridget had just come in, and fingers of cold air lingered in the kitchen. Thad sat opposite Muppy, studying at the table, and remembered thinking that it was good: hokey, but good. When the phone rang, he picked it up and, tilting back on two legs of his chair, said, "County morgue. You kill 'em, we chill 'em."

The voice on the other end was his father's, but somehow it wasn't. It sounded like a bad tape, or a poor imitation. It sounded strangled and terribly far away. "Put your mother on the phone."

Thad knew instinctively not to say anything, and handed the phone to his mother.

In those few seconds that it took for his mother to take the phone certain things dug into Thad's mind, and forever after, that day was marked by the drip of water into a mixing bowl in the sink and the sight of a teabag staining the drainboard. His mother's voice was spare as she said, "Yes, yes, I see. Yes, I'll come."

"I have to go out for a while. Have to meet your father. Something's come up . . . I . . . he. . . ." And the whole time she spoke, Ellen St. Clair was putting her coat on and gathering her pocketbook. "I don't know how long I'll be. If I'm not back in time, Bridget'll fix something . . . for supper and—"

"But Mom, where are you going? I mean what's the—"

Their mother stood in the doorway and the cold air rushed into the kitchen and seemed to take hold of all of them as she said, "I don't know. Your father wants me to meet him at the Tap Room. I. . . ." And she was gone, slipping across the driveway, over the crusts of ice and into the car. It wasn't until Thad saw the car turn out of the driveway and into the street, fitting itself neatly into the two black strips, that he realized the seriousness of it all: his mother, who was terrified of driving in ice, had gone out and driven away without even thinking about it.

Bridget fixed scrambled eggs, and Muppy didn't tell her how she hated eggs and would rather have peanut butter. Afterwards, they all put their dishes in the dishwasher and somehow the serving plate got done and the table wiped without anyone saying "That's your part" or "I did mine." Thad took out the garbage and stood for a moment looking up at the starless sky, then in at the two empty spaces in the garage where his mother's and father's cars ought to be. For the rest of the evening the three of them, Thad and Muppy and Bridget, sat huddled around the kitchen table as if leery of drifting off into other parts of the house.

Headlights arched past the kitchen door, and Thad heard first one car and then another crunch over the ice and come to a stop. His father burst through the door and across the kitchen to the hall, and Thad heard his footsteps on the stairs before his mother had gotten into the house. Ellen St. Clair closed the door and leaned against it. Her face was pinched and looked at once frail and strong as steel. She took off her coat and unwound a yellow muffler from her neck, and Thad remembered thinking that it left her looking like a plucked chicken. "OK, it's late and I want you all to go to bed. We'll talk tomorrow." She waited for a minute, standing by the open closet door and weaving the strands of wool from the scarf around her fingers. But her waiting was tense, and forebore any questions. "Yes, tomorrow. We'll talk tomorrow." And his mother turned and followed his father up the stairs, and all Thad could think of was that his father had gone up to bed wearing his overcoat and galoshes.

All night long there had been a steady hum of voices from his parents' room, and the next morning his father didn't get up. Thad saw him—this father

113

who strained to run the power mower at dawn on summer mornings and frequently was up before even Muppy on Christmas—as a hump of yellow blanket when his mother slipped out of the bedroom to go down for breakfast. When they had come home from school, their father had been there, wearing khakis and a sweater on a Wednesday and looking somehow diminished.

"Before you all go off in eighteen different directions, I want to talk to you—your mother and I do —in the kitchen, to get everything out in the open, lay it on the line. Come on everybody. . . ." His father's voice had started out strong, then dwindled. And in the end it was their mother who was left to deal with the children while their father pushed his way out of the kitchen and through the hall sending a bisque figurine from the table crashing onto the floor. And no one moved to pick it up.

And Thad was back in the present again. Back to the beach house that had a sudden feeling of emptiness. Back to the sounds from the bay, of powerboats and voices and the slap of water that swept through the windows and displaced the silence. Thad moved through the rooms. He flopped down on the floor next to Barney and wondered idly about his mother and Muppy, then remembered that they had mentioned going out to eat. It was as if the running was still going on inside of him, as if some kind of inner legs still churned and moved, the way Barney's legs twitched in sleep. And suddenly Thad was moving around the house, going from room to room again. For a few minutes he seemed not to be aware of what he was doing, as though the things piling up on the table were a continuance of his running. He stood back, checking the sleeping bag, the radio and flashlight and the citronella. Thad felt like a jogger stopped in traffic, felt as though he were running in place as he shoved several cans of soup and a loaf of bread and some apples into a knapsack. He fingered the straps and the worn softness of the cloth and remembered his first camping trip and how his father hadn't gone.

It had been the sixth-grade father-son camping trip. The school was given to father-son expeditions just as it was given to blue blazers and gray flannel pants. And Thad had been wildly excited. Some of his friends had already been camping and Thad envied them their knapsacks with the newness already worn off and wanted a brown sleeping bag like everybody else's. His father had entered grandly into the plans for the trip. Thad still felt the skin crawling up the back of his neck when he remembered his father coming home with bags and boxes of camping equipment from The Outdoor Man instead of from Sears or Ward's. But a few days before the trip, his father had made his excuses: "The office . . . something came up. . . . You know how it is . . . would if

I could. . . . golf tournament. . . ." His mother had taken everything back to the store for credit, gotten Thad a knapsack and sleeping bag, and sent him off with Jimmy Wilson and his father. At night around the campfire, Thad had moved close to Mr. Wilson and pretended to himself that he and Jimmy were brothers, and when he got home and his father said, "Hey, sport, how was the trip?" he had shrugged and said, "OK, I guess."

Adding a can of baked beans and a saucepan, he fastened the strap. He took one of Muppy's crayons and wrote on the back of an envelope, "Mom, don't worry. Back soon. Thad," and propped the note against the sugar bowl.

Thad worked his way back down Bayside Drive, alternately walking and jogging, but the running inside of him continued. His feet still seemed to hit the sidewalk, one and then the other, one and then. . . . He started across the walkway on the bridge, behind the metal grating that separated the traffic from the fishermen, stepping over tackle boxes and around buckets. He moved past the backsides of people leaning on the railing and dodged poles and fishhooks. The wind was hot and smelled of fish and exhaust fumes.

"Your father has made a mistake," Ellen St. Clair had said. And for a moment it seemed to Thad

116

as if that was all she was going to say. Just "Your father has made a mistake" hanging there over the kitchen table while Bridget played with the salt cellar and Muppy cracked her knuckles and Thad stared out the window at the steady drip of water from the roof.

And then she had gone on. "At work, at the Savings and Loan, when the auditors came in at the end of the fiscal year, they found withdrawals from dormant accounts . . . that were unauthorized." Thad noticed that his mother's voice was gaining momentum as though she wanted to spit it all out at once.

"They found this when confirmation letters were sent out and discrepancies were noted. This led to a further investigation, and yesterday the president of the company called your father in and—"

"What's unauthorized something of something?" asked Muppy, leaning her elbows on the table.

Thad saw his mother's fingers whiten around the knuckles as she clenched her hands and twisted them. "I'm sorry, Mup. Didn't mean to sound like a walking newspaper. What I mean is that there was money missing from the accounts that aren't used much, money that had been taken and—"

"And they think Daddy took it?" said Muppy, pushing her glasses higher on her nose.

117

"Yes, yes, I'm afraid they do and—"

"He didn't," said Muppy slipping down from the table. "He didn't," she said again before she left the room.

"But he did. He admits it and. . . ." Ellen St. Clair got up and went to the sink, filling the tea kettle, moving slowly and deliberately as if trying to gather the edges of herself together. And Thad, looking at his mother's back, wondered if he would ever be able to forgive his father for forcing their mother to stand alone in the kitchen and tell them this.

"But it's going to work out. Everything. It will— I know it," said his mother turning back to the table. "Oh, not right away. It will take time and . . . but can you imagine how much better your father feels knowing it's over and out in the open, knowing he made a mistake and. . . . There's a kind of relief just in admitting it and being ready to make—"

And the tea kettle had shrieked. It was as though they had reached a kind of plateau, as if now was the time for drinking tea and letting things rest a while.

Thad saw his father come into the kitchen. Saw him make himself a cup of instant coffee at the stove and stand with his back to the rest of them. He stood there, stirring the coffee, as if waiting to be invited to turn around, to join them at the table.

"Thadeus," his mother had said, leaning back

118

and touching her husband on the arm. "It's all right. We've talked about it, and the children understand. Everybody makes mistakes, and they understand."

The same voice inside of Thad sounded again. My father's a crook and they say I understand—and I don't. *I do not understand."*

Thad found himself across the bridge and standing at the intersection of the highway and the road to Watch Island. He didn't remember getting there but his shirt under the knapsack was soaked with sweat and his shoulder and the side of his face were hot from carrying the sleeping bag. He moved further down the road, out of the sun, and waited for a ride.

Thad wasn't sure that he had ever looked his father directly in the eye again after that day in the kitchen. There had seemed to follow months of looking over someone's shoulder and coming sideways into a room. It was a time of long pauses and half-finished sentences, of lurking in hallways and listening in the niche at the top of the steps. When he had been small, the cubbyhole was one of Thad's favorite places. It was a place to go at night after his mother had tucked him in, a place to curl up, surrounded on three sides by spindles, and listen to the voices and laughter coming from the downstairs, grown-up world. Thad had crouched there the night

119

his grandmother had come, but there had been no laughter that night and the voices had been sharp and jagged.

". . . disgrace to the family . . . the name of St. Clair . . . what you've done to the children . . . to think that you're my son. . . ." His grandmother's voice had been at once strident and imperious.

Thad heard his own mother's voice, and it was strong and low and seemed to lead his grandmother to the door. He heard the door close behind her. And the next day his mother told him and Bridget that when the time came she would take them into court—to be with their father. When the time came Thad had stayed home and vomited on the rug, and Bridget and his mother had gone alone.

The car stopped a few feet past him and Thad picked up the sleeping bag and ran for it. He remembered the things his mother had told him about hitchhiking, but the road ahead looked long and hot and he pulled open the door and climbed in.

"Going camping?" the man asked.

"Yes, sir, over on Watch Island. Drop me at the bridge, if you can."

"Not going alone, I hope." The car lurched along the road.

"No, uh-uh. Catching up with the group. I had to work and couldn't leave with everybody else."

"That's good. Bit of weather coming up, they say." And the car radio crackled sharply as if in affirmation. "Keep an eye out."

"Yes, sir, and thanks for the ride," said Thad as the man slowed the car.

He stood by the side of the road and looked up, and the sky was sharp and clear.

CHAPTER 12

The station wagon passed him at the hump of the bridge, then dropped down the other side and swung into the camp ground on Watch Island. From the back it looked like a circus car, wedged with people and grocery bags, with rolls of paper towels and boxes of Cheerios poking out of the top, with sleeping bags and folding aluminum chairs. A small boy made a face and waved at Thad out of the window, and plastered against the back of the car was a home-made sign that said, "The McHenrys—Watch Island or bust."

And for a minute Thad wanted to be a Mc-Henry.

He wanted to run and catch up and hurl himself into the car with these people he didn't even know.

He wanted to help them set up their tent and light their fire—these McHenrys who all seemed to be heading in the same direction, and who even now, stopped at the entrance, laughed and joked with the ranger.

Thad stood for a minute, looking, then veered to the right, pushing his way through the woods. He ducked past loblolly pines and scrub oaks, pulling his sleeping bag loose from low, gnarled branches and lifting his feet high out of the marsh grass. He emerged past the bend in the road, out of sight of the ranger, and headed south.

The dunes rose up on the left side of the road, blocking the view of the sea, but already the sky over the ocean was the darker blue that comes with late afternoon. The sun beat down on the marshlands on the west side of the island, and gulls screeched as they dropped to land then rose again. Thad dropped his sleeping bag and eased the knapsack on his shoulders, lifting the straps and letting the air hit the dampness of his shirt. He heard a car and jumped to the side of the road as the McHenry's station wagon pulled up next to him.

"Can we give you a lift?" asked the man at the wheel. "We're heading for campground C. Hop in if that'll help you any."

And suddenly the back door opened, and it was as if Thad were being sucked into a welter of arms and legs and cooler chests. His sleeping bag disappeared into the very back and the car door slammed.

"Jake McHenry," said the man at the wheel. "My wife, Joan, and that's the gang in back. Heading out alone?"

The "gang" consisted of four McHenry boys and a spotted dog, all of whom seemed to be shifting and rearranging themselves in the back of the car.

"Oh, huh, no sir. Just catching up with the group. I had to work and got off late. Just go as far as you're going and it's not far from there." And Thad found the story sliding easily off his tongue the second time. He counted on Mr. McHenry not to know that campground C was the last one down, that beyond that was the stretch of wild beach reaching down to the lighthouse on the point of the island.

Thad stood at the top of the dune looking back. Already the McHenrys seemed small and distant as they unloaded the car and started to set up their tent. He watched for another minute, then slid down the far side of the dune, landing in a heap at the bottom. He shrugged off the knapsack and flexed his shoulders. Kicking off his shoes, he tied the laces together and hung them around his neck. Then picking up his knapsack, he headed down the beach. Thad walked along the firm, wet sand near the water's edge, planting his feet down hard, then looking back at the trail of footprints. All around him the beach was deserted. The dunes, forming a barrier at the back of the beach, were hemmed with faded red snow fences, and the tough sea grass bent in the breeze.

Finding a natural hollow between two dunes, Thad dropped his sleeping bag and knelt to unload his knapsack. He flattened out a shelf of sand and lined his canned goods and canteen in a row. Then he scouted around for pieces of dry driftwood and laid a fire. Flopping down against the side of the dune, he scooped out a sand chair with his back, making for himself a kind of throne facing out to sea.

Thad stared at the ocean, trying to blank his mind, to smooth it over, to whitewash it as though it were a fence. He wanted to set out his thoughts, to sort and shuffle them, wanted, in a way, to become sure of what he was thinking: to pin things down, to anchor the corners, the way the McHenrys were securing their tent while he had stood on the top of the dune and watched.

But still the feeling of running had hold of him. His legs shifted restlessly against the beach, and he dug his heels into the sand until he felt dampness. Thad jumped up and ran in a large loop, circling down to the edge of the water so that the waves hit the legs of his jeans, then back up to the hollow, flopping down into his niche.

The thoughts he had tried to outrun came down around him, and Thad was surprised to find his fists were clenched and shoved down deep into the sand.

It had been the feeling of weakness in his father that had shaken Thad.

There had been times when his mother had

spoken of mistakes and sorrow and restitution that Thad had wanted to accept it. He had been reaching out and waiting to accept—if only his father had taken hold of things, if only his father had stood firm, turning things around and moving forward.

But in those months after he had been found out, Thadeus St. Clair had seemed to recede, to diminish, to crouch inward until even the everyday seemed to go on without him. And Thad had learned to change the washers in the sink and unclog the drains while his father stared out the window and waited for dinner.

Thad pulled the transistor radio out of the knapsack and switched it on, pushing the volume up high. Static rushed and crackled out at him and he spun the dial. There was the faint sound of music webbed over with static, and he turned the radio off. He remembered the man in the car talking of a bit of weather and suddenly he thought of Muppy: Muppy and Tru-weather and the way she was afraid of storms. He wondered what she was doing and if she missed him. He looked up at the sky, still clear but edged all around with a funny bleached-yellow look.

Daylight seemed to be slipping out from under him. The water darkened, and the air was suddenly cool. It was as though the cold came from somewhere inside of him, the way he had felt once when a fiery new sunburn had glazed him over with heat and the inside of him had shivered. Thad began to think of lighting the fire, of heating the baked beans, when he heard the sound of a four-wheel drive bouncing along the road in back of the dunes. He crouched down against the beach, willing the ranger to keep going, to go to the lighthouse and turn around, coming back by road and not swinging around and driving up the shore. No camping was allowed on this part of the beach and Thad stayed flat, his mind racing. He thought of the McHenrys—of the boys in the back of the station wagon—and decided that if the ranger came he would say he was one of them. "Family up in campground C . . . Just wandered down here for a little quiet . . . name of McHenry." And for a minute Thad wished that it were so. When the jeep ground back up the road, he felt a twinge of disappointment.

He ate cold soup and baked beans and bread and washed it down with root beer. He dawdled over the meal, stretching it out mouthful by mouthful, pushing the bread around the insides of the cans, cleaning his spoon in the surf and drying it on the seat of his jeans. He walked along the shore until the land jutted inwards, then came back to the campsite. The sun had dropped out of sight in the west, and daylight hung suspended briefly, then began to slither away. Thad leaned back against the dune.

He had come here, running even when he was walking or riding in a car, to sort things out. He had come for a thinking time, and now that he was confronted with it, he didn't want it.

He found his mind scuttling backwards and sideways like a hermit crab. Instinctively his legs moved against the sand.

His father lay on the kitchen floor and cried like a baby: great gulping baby sobs, gasping sobs that choked and sputtered. And in between he said, "I didn't mean to do it. . . I'm sorry, sorry, sorry. . . ."

They had been having supper, eating tuna casserole in the kitchen, Thad remembered. And Bridget had been badgering their mother to let her use the car though the night was bad and Ellen St. Clair had already said no a dozen times. Thad remembered that his mother had looked tired, and almost beaten, that she had turned to their father for support and that he had shrugged and taken another helping of casserole.

Something inside of Thad had broken, and he had lashed out at his father the way one would scold a child. "You've got tuna fish on your chin," Thad had said, his voice shot through with disgust. His father had dropped his fork and fallen onto his knees, swaying there while great sobs rose up inside of him. Then he had slid crying onto the floor. The last thing Thad had seen, before he ran, had been his mother kneeling on the floor cradling her husband's head in her arms. And Thad had known, as he stood on the far side of his bedroom door, that he had goaded his father into this, the way one would bully a smaller child—one who wouldn't fight back.

Then immediately Thad's mind seemed to dart sideways, picking up other thoughts, other memories.

There had been the time in sixth grade when Miss Bracken had unjustly accused Thad of cheating on a math exam, and his father had taken off from work the next day to go with Thad so that he could explain it all and vindicate himself. It wasn't so much that his father had said anything, but his being there had given Thad courage to speak out, to prove his honesty. Then the scene shifted: he was a younger Thad, and for some reason he remembered sitting on his father's shoulders during the St. Patrick's Day parade, remembered the feeling of power and strength that had given him: a steady untottering feeling that lasted long after the parade was over.

Darkness pulled in around him. He dug matches out of his pocket and lit the driftwood, watching it flare up briefly, then settle down, hoping the ranger wouldn't spot it as being beyond the campground. Thad thought again of the McHenrys together in their tent. He unrolled his sleeping bag and climbed inside, scrunching around until he dug hollows in the sand to fit his body. Thad lay still. He watched the sky, tracing the sweep of light from the

129

lighthouse as it arced the sky. Around and around
—light and dark and light again. A mosquito buzzed
and he pulled the edge of the sleeping bag up over
his head.

And through his sleep his legs ached from running, running, running, and fought against the sleeping bag.

Thad woke up the next morning tired and
chilled. The sky was dark, a leaden gray, and over-
cast. Silence seemed to be pulled taut round him,
and on the top of it he heard the jeep moving up
the road. Last night's fire was shriveled black. Thad
stretched, trying to uncramp his muscles, and his
head landed in the sand. Crawling out of the sleeping bag, he stood up and brushed at his head with
his hands, sending a shower of sand down around
him.

Slowly Thad moved down the beach. Everything was outlined in shades of gray: the sand, the
sky, the tufts of grass. The ocean looked mean and
black, and waves beat against the shore, pushing up
and cutting into the sand. Thad walked into the edge
of the surf, and the water that swirled around his
feet was strangely warm. The wind pushed against
his back, and for a minute he was almost running.

When he turned to go back up the beach he
was facing into the wind. Thad stood for a minute
as if pinned there in space, then dropping his head,

he tunneled his way back to his place against the dune. He dropped down out of the wind and leaned against the sand. He searched the sky, and in spite of its ominous look, inertia seemed to have taken hold of him as he sat there as if waiting for some kind of resolution.

Yesterday's restlessness had spent itself.

After a while he opened a can of vegetable soup and ate it cold, swallowing whole the bits of carrots and celery and scooping great mounds of sand around him with the empty can.

Out of the howling of the wind above him Thad thought he heard his name. He rubbed his eyes and felt them gritty with sand, then heard it again.

"Thad-eeee-ussss."

As he pulled himself up out of the hollow between the dunes, the northeast wind smacked him in the face. He blinked and started to duck down, then looked again.

His mother was coming across the beach, pushed along by the wind, her hair standing out around her face, clutching a white bakery bag in the crook of her arm.

Ellen St. Clair dropped down on the sleeping bag next to her son. For a moment neither of them said anything, then his mother pushed the hair out of her eyes and handed the paper bag to him.

Thad bit into a doughnut, and the taste of honey replaced and overcame the taste of cold vegetable soup.

131

CHAPTER 13

"This is the way a beach ought to look," said Ellen St. Clair, handing the last doughnut to Thad and crumpling the paper bag.

"Yeah, specially when I have my doughnuts hand delivered." Thad licked his fingers.

"No pizza parlors, no soft ice cream, plenty of shells," his mother's voice drifted on. "I keep meaning to come out here to swim . . . if it weren't so far. . . . Of course I'd have to remember to bring a jug of iced tea, or hot coffee." She shuddered slightly and pulled at the zipper of her windbreaker. "We could come for the day sometime and bring Muppy, but I guess Bridget wouldn't. . . ."

And for a minute it seemed to Thad as if it were the most natural thing in the world for him

132

and his mother to be sitting on the beach at Watch Island idly talking, with a storm coming up.

"Have to do it on my day off," his mother went on. "We can bring lunch . . . just have to remember who I loaned my cooler chest to."

"Bridget probably took it and gave it to somebody for a beer party or something."

"No, I seem to remember . . . somebody's vacation—they needed the cooler for. . . ."

A sandpiper skirted the water's edge, then turned and darted across the beach on little stick legs.

Like we're doing, thought Thad. Mom and I come close to things then turn and run away. He watched the sandpiper, saw it skimming the beach as though propelled by the wind. And Thad knew that his mother would sit there and outwait him while the wind blew harder and they talked about cooler chests and picnics.

Thad reached for the empty tin cans and stuffed them back in his knapsack. He opened a can of root beer and held it out to his mother.

"Yuh, no, thanks. You have it."

Taking a deep swallow he wiped his mouth on the back of his hand and pushed the base of the can down into the sand, twisting it firmly in place as though the wind might lift it and carry it away.

"OK Mom," said Thad, concentrating on reloading the knapsack, "you came because . . . how'd you know? I mean—"

"Well, it wasn't hard to figure out. I knew you hadn't run away. The note said. . . . You just needed a little thinking time, I guess, an uncrowding, kind of. And then when I saw your camping stuff was gone too. . . ."

"Boy, I'd never make it in the CIA, would I?" said Thad, leaning forward to look for the sandpiper.

"Oh, and I checked with the ranger last night. He scouted around and got back to me. He said he'd keep his eye on you. I would have let you stay awhile, but with this hurricane on its way heading up the coast. Veering out to sea I hope, but I decided I'd better. . . ."

Thad felt his face go red, felt it suddenly hot in spite of the wind at the thought of his mother checking with the ranger. Checking up on him as though he were a kid. He stood up quickly, facing into the wind. The sky lowered around him, and the word "hurricane" caught up and overtook him. He dropped back onto the sand, facing his mother across the burnt out fire.

"Hurricane?" His voice cracked, and for once Thad didn't try to stop it.

"Hurricane? But what about Muppy? And the way she's scared of weather? I mean a regular storm is bad enough, but a hurricane. Does she know? Has she—"

"Relax Thad," said his mother, crumbling a

134

piece of charred wood between her fingers then digging her hand into the sand to clean them. "Bridget's with her. When I left they were putting tape crisscrossed on the windows just in case. Sometimes it helps to do things."

"Has she listened to Tru-weather?"

"Oh yes, Tru-weather was going a mile a minute."

"Funny kid. Weird. Why does she care? About weather and all and listening to Tru-weather as if it were a regular show?"

"I think it has something to do with her internal weather. It's been pretty rough you know, since your father went to prison."

There it was, thought Thad. Out in the open, what they had been skirting and darting at like the sandpiper.

"Well, yeah, it's been rough on her—worse for her probably."

"I don't know about worse," said Ellen St. Clair. "It hasn't been easy for you and Bridget either, and you have to remember that everyone has a different way of dealing with something. But for Muppy I think it's a kind of instability. As if nothing were certain any more. Tottery."

"So she sees it like the weather?" Thad asked. "Like always being on the verge of a storm, that any minute everything might change, and then turn dark and—"

"I think that's it," said his mother, getting up. "Let's walk a bit. The storm seems to be holding back."

They started down the beach. The wind was to their backs and everything around them seemed to be in a state of suspension. The clouds, low and heavy, were held pressed against the sky, and the black and angry ocean had a muffled sound.

"For the rest of us," his mother went on, pulling the hood of her windbreaker up over her head and tying it, "probably the hardest part was that stretch of time between the discovery of what happened and the actual sentencing—even the actual day he left."

Thad remembered, and was forced back into those months of restlessness, of agitation, when his father walked the house. It was a time of jangled nerve endings and feelings as tender as new skin, pink and raw. Thad remembered his father sitting idly, like an old man on a park bench, with his hands dropped between his knees, then leaving the house abruptly, going for long, aimless walks. Thad had felt excluded that his father hadn't asked him to go, but had known at the time that he would not have gone.

"For us they were endless months," said Ellen St. Clair, picking up his thoughts. "But Muppy saw it even then as her father still being home—of life going on. A continuity."

"And she was above or below the rest of it," said Thad, standing still and feeling the pull of the undertow against his legs as he dug his toes into the sand.

"Yes, and for Muppy the worst time was when your father left—when they took him away—"

"And that's when it started, the weather, and Tru-weather, and being afraid of thunder and watching the sky. . . ."

"Yes," said his mother, "that's when it started."

A wave caught Thad on the side of the leg and he ran up onto the beach. "And the *Grimm's*," he called into the wind. "That started then too—reading the stories and counting the days."

"That's right. It's a kind of coping. A way of handling things." Ellen St. Clair ducked around to the leeward side of the lighthouse, leaning against the weathered stone. "Last night she read *The Riddling Tree*. You know how serious she can get. She kept wondering if because the story was so short it still counted, and when she went to bed she was still trying to decide if that was good enough or if she should tack another one on."

Thad laughed and heard the laughter echo roundly in that wedge of silence out of the wind. He tugged at a piece of marsh grass and felt it dig into his fingers. He turned abruptly, facing his mother. "I wasn't running away. But I was running just the same." And he headed back into the wind.

137

His face, buffeted by the wind, was numb and his ears felt enormous. There was a roaring inside his head. His mouth tasted of salt, and his eyes were slits. Thad dropped back, catching his mother by the arm, and together they worked their way to the side of the dune and sat down. The wind skimmed the tops of their heads.

"It's picking up a bit; we'd better head back. Last I heard, the storm was veering out to sea, but was due to pass this way sometime." Ellen St. Clair checked her watch and looked at the sky.

Thad stopped rolling the sleeping bag and said suddenly, "But how can you stand it? Everything that's happened, and will happen?"

His mother took the sleeping bag out of his hands and finished rolling it. She tied the strings, and for a minute Thad wasn't sure she was going to answer him.

"I don't know if I can explain it. I'm not sure if I understand it all myself. It's the kind of thing that makes me envy people who have the answers in neat little packages there for everyone to see, when all I have seems to come from the inside out. A kind of knowing. It has to do, I guess, with what changes and what doesn't change, and with how we grab hold of that changing and that staying the same."

She settled back against the dune, pulling her knees toward her. "Has to do with what's variable

138

and what's constant. Like this island." Ellen St. Clair leaned forward suddenly.

"If we came back tomorrow, or next week, or next summer, the shore line would be different— worn away or built up. Gouged out, the dunes would be shifted or flattened, or new ones made— from the storm or the tide, or just general attrition. But underneath it all it's still Watch Island—that doesn't change. The way I've worked it out for myself, and maybe you won't see it that way, is that when your father and I got married we made pledges—promises—and those pledges are our kind of Watch Island. That part that doesn't change. The constant. Though I must confess," she said laughing, "that it's taken its share of gouging this year. But don't you see, Thad, it's still there. That's the important part. That's what counts."

Thad felt as though he had been fed too much too fast. He felt overstuffed. Instinctively, he swallowed. "But why is it all on you? How about . . . I mean—"

"If you mean your father and me, the promises we made were two-way. This is something I refuse to give up on. It's what I believe. What I hang on to." Ellen St. Clair untied the strings on the sleeping bag and tied them over again. "There have been mistakes. Your father—" And abruptly she stopped, and for a time Thad was only aware of the sound of the wind.

139

"No. No, Thad." His mother's voice seemed to be thrust out upon him. "Not a mistake. Your father did something wrong. Very wrong. He committed a crime. He stole. Maybe our—or my—mistake was in insisting on calling it a mistake—in never letting you and Bridget and Muppy really come to grips with it. Yes, Thad, it was wrong and. . . ."

And Thad felt as though a host of unasked questions had been answered.

His mother went on. "A wrong has been done and restitution made, and is still being made, and will be made for a long time to come. Now it's time for going forward. And Thadeus, you've got to believe it's not one-sided. Your father and I have talked, all these months, and now by letter. . . ."

Thad remembered the voices that had gone on long into the night, remembered going to sleep to the rhythm of his parents' voices from behind their closed bedroom door.

He pushed his remembering aside and caught up with his mother's conversation. Her words seemed scattered now, dispersed by the wind.

"Things will be different, but there are certain built-in problems. The St. Clair name for one. You know. Thad, a name is an asset and a liability. Your father's mother saw it all out of proportion, saw the name as an asset but never gave her son the strength to go with it. I'm not trying to influence you against your grandmother, but—"

"Why didn't she stick by him?" Thad asked. "Why did she turn on her own son and—"

"I don't know—can't be sure. But your father was hurt. When it reached the point where she cared more for the name than the person. . . ."

Thad heard his mother's voice rise and fall, a counterpoint against the wind, and while she spoke he could almost believe that things were going to be different.

Thad struggled into the knapsack and tightened the straps. His mother picked up the sleeping bag. She paused and said, "You've learned a bit, I think, about the liability of a name, haven't you, Thad?"

He ducked his head and kicked at the remains of last night's fire. "How did you know?"

"After we got home last night and found your note, I went up to the House of Terror to see if you were still there. Saw that man called Carl," she said, and Thad thought he saw his mother shudder. "He told me how you had walked out—had quit."

"Yeah, but it was because—"

"He also told me about the name—about Brook Sinclair."

"It wasn't that. I'm not sure if I meant to—"

"And about the check," his mother went on. "You've lost your job, Thad, but you earned your money. If you take the check back to Carl, he'll

141

give you a new one with the proper name on it: your proper name. It's what you do with a name that counts. It's up to you to make a name for yourself. Come on, let's hurry; it's starting to rain."

As they passed campground C, Thad peered through the rain-streaked windshield, but the Mc-Henry's car was gone. The camp was empty.

CHAPTER 14

There is a time towards the end of August when the sky takes on an almost autumn look, a kind of flattening, but softer, with the sun lacking the glare of midsummer. And this reaching-into-fall is more noticeable in the early morning and late afternoon.

Thad sat in a sand chair on the dock with his breakfast spread out around him. He finished a bowl of cereal and spooned the dregs of the sweet-ish-warm milk into his mouth, then started in on a peanut butter and banana sandwich, washing it down with alternating swallows of orange juice and root beer. He shooed a fly off a sticky bun and polished an apple on the front of his shirt.

The air was clear, bringing the other side of the bay sharply into focus. Thad studied layers of blue sky, the green of pine trees, and the deeper blue of the water. Across the way Peter came up out of the cabin and stood on the stern of the *Sea Hunter*. He waved and shouted. "Be right over." He heard the drone of boats further out on the bay and the sound of voices from inside the house.

Bridget and his mother called to one another with the insistence of people getting ready to go someplace. "Has the dryer stopped yet? . . . Put it in my pocketbook. . . . Don't forget the . . . Watch the time."

Sunlight glimmered on the bay, and for a while Thad tried to pin his eyes on a spot in the channel, but the water churned and pulled beneath the surface, moving on relentlessly. It was as though the summer ran before him like the current, briefly in view, then sliding out of reach. There were the parts that made it every year: the ocean with its sand and silence, the stillness of the late afternoon heat, the slap of flip-flops on the boardwalk, and the smell of coconut in suntan oil. There were gulls and crabs and horseshoe crabs. French fries and pizza and the music of the merry-go-round. There was the quiet of the bay at night; there were stars, and in the distance, the car headlights on the mainland bridge.

And there were the particularities that would forever after mark this summer and set it apart: Muppy with the book of *Grimm's* on her head or

144

wrapped in a towel or under her pillow. The House of Terror, with paper maché rocks and plastic moss, and Carl's gauze shirt open on a chest that was white and hairless. There was Bridget crying on the sofa, and the picture of Thadeus Brook St. Clair splashed across the paper.

There was Peter: part of every summer, but also very much a part of this summer—that was like no other.

And there was his mother sitting on the beach at Watch Island eating doughnuts and talking—measuring her talk against the darkness of the sky. And Thad found, because of her coming, because of her talking, that gradually his legs no longer thrashed against the sheets at night. And the running stopped.

Barney pushed against the screen with his nose and wedged his paw between the door and the frame, working his way through the opening. He scoured the dock for crumbs and licked the inside of the cereal bowl before flopping down next to Thad.

"Where were you last night when I needed you, Barney?" asked Thad out loud, wiping his hands on the dog's thick coat.

Thad thought how he could have used Barney the night before. Barney, or anybody. Somebody. Even Muppy. He thought back to how he almost hadn't made it all the way to the House of Terror, had almost stopped part way, as he had done twice before, edging away and backtracking and losing himself in the surge of people on the boardwalk. Then he thought about coming home.

But last night Thad had pushed his way on, past the Pizza Parlor and the funny mirrors and the Candy Corner. He had forced himself around to the alley where the dumpsters swarmed with flies and Carl sat on the unpainted step.

Thad had rehearsed the words, flipping sentences in his head like so many index cards, but instead he had pulled the rumpled check out of his pocket and held it out.

Carl took another drag on his cigarette and flicked it into the alley. He rose slowly, without saying anything, took the check, scratched his stomach, and disappeared into the back door of the snack bar next door.

Thad had stood holding on to the ground with his feet, fighting off the feeling of panic. In the distance he heard the race and dip of the Wild Mouse and the sound of screams.

Then Carl was back, holding a new check out to him, tearing the other into bits and dropping it onto the ground.

"Thanks," said Thad, turning away from Carl's face, which looked at once swarmy and weaseled.

"OK Sinclair."

146

Stopping at the end of the alley, Thad turned and called, "Not Sinclair. It's St. Clair. Thad St. Clair."

The voices inside the house heightened, and Thad knew it was almost time for his mother and Bridget to leave for Allenwood to visit his father.

Thad and his mother had somehow worked their way around the idea of the trip, circling it and viewing it sideways and upside down and finally head on. And it was Ellen St. Clair who finally decided that Thad wasn't ready to go, that Thad would stay home and take care of Muppy. And when Pat and Bill had left to go to college orientation and had handed the beach stand over to Thad, that had settled it all the more firmly.

Thad dragged his feet out from under Barney and draped them over the dog's body. He took the envelope out of his pocket and smoothed it out.

Last night, after he had come home from the House of Terror, Thad had written to his father. The letter hadn't come easily, with his pen stubbing against words and slipping over thoughts. He had stopped and started and crumpled sheets of paper. He had erased and blotched and crisscrossed words.

Finally Thad had written about the weather and the beach stand, about the fins he was going to buy and about Barney swimming in the bay. He wrote

"Hurry home" and "See you soon" and signed it "Miss ya." He folded the letter and stuffed it in the envelope. He held the pen tight for a minute and then scrawled DAD on the envelope.

Thad stared down at the envelope, while Barney sat up and nudged his arm with his nose. Thad knew that he didn't actually mean everything that was in the letter, didn't mean it all the way through.

But he wanted to mean it. Wanted it with all his being. That had to count for something. And somehow, inside of himself, Thad thought that by the time his father came home he would mean it.

His mother leaned over the railing and called down to him. "We're ready, Thad. Have to get on the road. Meet us around back, and I'll give you some emergency money and the telephone number of the motel where we'll spend the night."

Peter arrived on a bike, letting it fall with a clank against the side of the house.

Barney climbed in the car and had to be dragged out. Bridget threw the suitcases into the back, and Muppy came out with a milk carton full of shells for her father.

Ellen St. Clair rolled down the window and leaned out. "Take care of Muppy, and lock the doors tonight. We'll see you late tomorrow."

She started the engine and put the car in reverse. Silently, without saying anything, Thad held out the letter.

His mother took it and dropped it into her canvas bag. She looked at Thad, her eyes holding his. "Thanks, Thad." And the car swung backwards into the street.

Muppy jumped up and down in front of him. "Come on, Thad. Let's go to the beach. It's time to open the stand. Remember, you said I could help. I'll get the towels. Come on, Thad, let's go. You don't think it'll rain, do you? Tru-weather said. . . ." She darted into the house.

The beach was starting to fill up. The sun beat down, and the lifeguard peeled off his sweat shirt and put on a straw hat.

Thad unlocked the large white bin at the side of the boardwalk, and together he and Muppy and Peter unloaded mats and folding chairs. They checked the book and counted out the umbrellas. Thad threw a couple over his shoulder and headed for the crest of the beach. Muppy marked the spots, making X's on the sand with her toe, and Thad threw the sticks, straightening them and snapping the umbrellas open. He walked back to get more, swiveling slightly on the balls of his feet.

When the umbrellas were lined in a row across the front of the beach, Thad checked the chart and sent Muppy running back with folding chairs.

"Hey Thad," she said coming back, "how much are you going to pay me? Don't forget, you said. . . . Now can I use a mat? Oh, and Thad, those girls—the ones that were here yesterday looking at you—they're here again. Over that way, LOOK."

Thad shoved a green surf mat at Muppy and headed her for the ocean. "Be careful and watch out now, OK?"

He sat down next to Peter and took off his shirt. Out of the corner of his eye he saw the girls. Two of them, fourteen or maybe fifteen. He put on his sun-glasses.

"Well, what do you think?" said Thad.

"Yeah. OK, Very OK," said Peter.

Thad looked at the girls again. He checked the sun and looked out toward the ocean and thought how there was a little over a week of summer left.